He's just a man! she told herself, but that didn't stop a tremble in the pit of her stomach as he looked around the room, dark eyes taking in the newcomer, his head nodding in acknowledgement, his eyes holding hers—a second or two, no more—and causing heat to sear downwards through her body.

'So, we have a stranger in our midst,' said this man who was causing the problems, his voice reverberating through her like the echoes of carillon bells. 'And you are…?'

'Marni Graham, sir,' she said, hoping she sounded more in control than she felt.

'In here I'm Gaz—just Gaz, Marni Graham,' he said. 'Welcome to the team.'

She really should say something—respond in some way—but her voice was lost somewhere in the general muddle of the new and unbelievably vital sensations she was experiencing right now.

Lust at first sight?

It can't be, Marni argued with herself—but silently, and very weakly.

The man in question had pulled his mask up to cover his nose and mouth and seemed about to turn away, but before he did he smiled at her.

Of course she couldn't see the smile, not on his lips, but she was certain it was there, shining in his eyes and making her feel warm and very, very unsettled.

Dear Reader

My fascination for desert regions still has me in its grip, so it's not surprising this is another book set in one of those fascinating places.

People ask where my ideas come from and I really cannot answer that. It seems to me that they come not as a full-blown notion but as little snippets of this and that. Some of these snippets came as I walked on a beach with Marion Lennox, a dear friend and a tremendous support from the day I started writing. So there we were, coming up from the beach through the native shrub, where I *know* bad snakes are known to lurk. Being terrified of snakes, I talked to keep my mind off it, prattling on about a young woman who was brought up by her grandfather, and as I talked they came to life in my head and their journey stretched before them.

As always, it didn't follow the original path, but hopefully the path it did follow proves enjoyable for you.

Meredith Webber

DATE WITH A SURGEON PRINCE

BY
MEREDITH WEBBER

First published in Great Britain 2013
by Mills & Boon, an imprint of Harlequin (UK) Limited,
Large Print edition 2014
Eton House, 18-24 Paradise Road,
Richmond, Surrey, TW9 1SR

© 2013 Meredith Webber

ISBN: 978 0 263 23882 2

Harlequin (UK) Limited's policy is to use papers that are natural, renewable and recyclable products and made from wood grown in sustainable forests. The logging and manufacturing processes conform to the legal environmental regulations of the country of origin.

Printed and bound in Great Britain
by CPI Antony Rowe, Chippenham, Wiltshire

Meredith Webber says of herself, 'Once I read an article which suggested that Mills & Boon® were looking for new Medical Romance™ authors. I had one of those "I can do that" moments, and gave it a try. What began as a challenge has become an obsession—though I do temper the "butt on seat" career of writing with dirty but healthy outdoor pursuits, fossicking through the Australian Outback in search of gold or opals. Having had some success in all of these endeavours, I now consider I've found the perfect lifestyle.'

Recent titles by Meredith Webber:

ONE BABY STEP AT A TIME
CHRISTMAS WHERE SHE BELONGS
THE SHEIKH AND THE SURROGATE MUM
NEW DOC IN TOWN*
ORPHAN UNDER THE CHRISTMAS TREE*
MELTING THE ARGENTINE DOCTOR'S HEART
TAMING DR TEMPEST

Christmas at Crystal Cove

These books are also available in eBook format from www.millsandboon.co.uk

PROLOGUE

'Are you completely mad? Bonkers? Round the twist?'

It wasn't often Marni yelled at her grandfather. In fact, if she'd been in any fit state to think about it, she'd have realised it was probably the first time. But this was just too much.

'It says here the man's a prince. Just because he hasn't married doesn't mean he'll be interested in some cockamamie story about being betrothed to me when he was three!'

She was still yelling, and brandishing the newspaper Pop had been reading at the same time, while the voice that lived in *her* head told her it would be a bad idea to bash an ailing eighty-four-year-old man to death, especially as she loved him to bits and couldn't bear the thought of life without him.

Except that she had to start—start imagining

it, that was. Eighty-four, with a blocked valve in his heart and blocked stents in the vital arteries that fed the heart muscle.

The specialist wanted to do open-heart surgery to replace the valve and, at the same time, the surgery necessary to bypass the stents. Pop was vacillating, another cause for anger because as a nurse she thought he should have the operation. Of course he should, he was a man who enjoyed life, and, selfishly perhaps, she really, really didn't want him dying of heart failure.

'You finished?' Pop retrieved the flapping paper from her now limp grasp, and opened it up to fold it at a different page. 'For your information, he was six, *you* were three. Now, look at this page near the back.'

Ignoring a momentary pang that she could no longer see the photo of the strong-featured face, framed by a white headdress, that had started the conversation, she peered over Pop's shoulder to read what he was showing her.

Not that her mind would take in much—she was still struggling with the little gem the old man had delivered earlier, finger pointing at the picture, voice full of wonder as he'd said, 'That's Ghazi. His father and I pledged the two of you would marry. Says here he's still single. You should get in touch.'

Forget this prince business and get with it, the inner voice in her head said firmly. Pop's made it clear he doesn't want you hanging around here while he's getting over the op, no matter how much you might want to be with him. Perhaps a short contract job somewhere else?

'See,' Pop was saying, and for a moment Marni wondered if he could hear her thoughts because he was pointing at a job advertisement. 'Theatre nurses wanted for new children's hospital in Ablezia. That might be why Ghazi's out here. He's looking for nurses.'

Yeah, right, she thought. Of course the crown prince of any country would have to check out hospital staff!

But Marni ignored the voice in her head this time, intent on reading exactly what was on offer in this place she'd never heard of, which, presumably, was far enough away from the Gold Coast, Queensland, Australia for her not to be tempted to ignore Pop's plea to keep away while he went through his operation.

If he went through with the operation!

Six months' contract' extendable, the advertisement read, air fares and accommodation provided. Six months would bring her up to Christmas and if Pop had the operation as soon as possible, then he'd be well on the way to recovery by the time she got home.

Six months! It was the answer to the other problem plaguing her too—her virginity! Given six months, thousands of miles from home—*surely* in six months she'd meet *someone*...

She sighed as she looked blankly at the paper, sighing because the virginity thing, as she thought of it, shouldn't really be a problem. It wasn't as if she'd held onto it deliberately, she'd just put things off for various reasons—Pop, Nelson, her mother's behaviour—then the cruel words of the last man she'd become involved with had made her realise it was a burden as well as an embarrassment.

Read the ad!

The pay scale seemed staggeringly generous,

but it was the thumbnail description of the country that made her heart flutter. Set by the warm waters of the Ablezian Sea, the country was well known for its underwater wonders—coral rccfs, abundant marine life, nesting turtles on the beaches...

This idea could actually solve some problems. She could make Pop happy by taking the job and getting out of the way while he recovered, make him even happier by at least meeting this prince guy—she owed Pop that much—and maybe, as a bonus, find someone with whom to have a holiday romance, or a work romance, or even just a little fling...

'I'll get the picture,' Pop said.

Marnie lost herself in thoughts of diving into warm gulf waters and playing with the fish and turtles. She barely heard Pop as he left the paper in front of her at the breakfast table and disappeared into his study.

Nelson, who'd been with her grandfather as long as Marni could remember, as valet, butler, cook and probably secretary, appeared in his usual silent way.

'I don't know, Nelson,' she said quietly. 'It seems wrong to even think of going away. Pop's taken care of me and been there for me all these years, surely now I can be there for him?'

Nelson shook his head.

'You know he probably won't have the op if you're around, because he doesn't want you to see him weak and sick. He wants you to remember him as the strong, active man he's always been, and can be again. He's far more likely to agree to the procedure if he knows you're not fretting over him.'

Nelson paused then, with only the slightest quaver in his voice, continued, 'You know I'll take good care of him.'

Blinking back the tears that had filled her eyes, Marni got to her feet and hugged the man she'd known since the age of two, when she'd been dumped on her grandfather because her mother's third husband hadn't wanted a kid around the place.

'I know you will, Nelson, and I know you're right about him recovering more quickly if I'm out of the way. If he's so set on me leaving, I'll do it. I'll take this job and check out this prince bloke, say hi to him from Pop, and report back. Can't you just imagine it—me rocking up to a palace in the desert to tell the local ruler he's betrothed to me! I'd be arrested and thrown into the deepest, darkest dungeon, or fitted with a straitjacket, or at the very least deported on the first plane out.'

Nelson's serious brown eyes studied her for a moment.

'It would make your grandfather very happy if you did meet the guy,' he said, so seriously that Marni groaned.

'Not you too!' she protested.

'Well, he was a really nice little kid and he was very good to you, although in those days you were a right little tantrum-throwing madam.'

'I met him? I knew him? When was all this?'

Marni frowned, trying to remember, to place a time she might have played with a prince.

Not something everyone would forget!

'It was shortly after you first arrived to live with us,' Nelson explained. 'Your grandfather had only recently moved into this apartment and

Ghazi's father booked out the entire hotel section for himself, his family and his staff.'

'The whole hotel?'

'He had a lot of wives and daughters,' Nelson said, as if that explained everything.

The Palazzo Versace was the first six-star hotel built on the Gold Coast, her grandfather's apartment one of a few privately owned condominiums included in the ritzy complex. As residents, they were free to make use of all the hotel facilities, the beautiful pools, the restaurants and the day spa, so she'd often played with the children of hotel guests as she had been growing up.

But one called Ghazi?

She had no memory of it at all, even when Pop returned with a box of photos showing her as a very small child with a boy who stood much taller. The photos told her they'd had fun together, two children at play while slender, black-robed figures sat in the shade by the pool.

'This is the one,' Pop, who'd been sifting through the photos, declared.

He handed it to her.

It was a more formal shot showing a tidily

dressed little girl, blonde hair in pigtails, pale blue eyes looking up at the boy sitting on the arm of one of the big lounge chairs in the hotel's foyer—a white-robed boy, who was holding her hand and smiling down at her.

Even then you could tell he was going to be good looking, although the miniature white head-dress he was wearing in the photo concealed all but his profile. Strong nose and jaw, a high fore-head, shapely lips widened in a slight smile—

'Hey, I was looking at that,' Marni protested as Pop turned the photo over.

He ignored her, pointing at the writing on the back. The top line was in his handwriting and, sure enough, there was this nonsense about the two of them being betrothed, Pop's signature at the end of the statement.

Beneath that was a line of beautiful, flowing, Arabic script, and presumably another signature.

'Honestly, Pop, you can't read Arabic so for all you know the man's written something like, "This nonsense should make the man happy!"'

Marni regretted her words the moment they'd popped out of her mouth and she caught the hurt in her grandfather's eyes, hurt that prompted a quick hug and a totally impulsive promise to go right now and apply for the job in a country called Ablezia.

'*And* I'll do my best to see this guy but only if you agree to have the operation,' Marni added. 'Deal?'

'Deal!' Pop agreed, and they shook on it, the slight tremble in her grandfather's hand reminding her just how frail he had become.

CHAPTER ONE

WAS IT THE subtle scent that perfumed the warm air—salt, spices, a fruit she couldn't identify—or the air itself that wrapped around her like the finest, softest, mohair blanket? Or was it the mind-boggling beauty of a landscape of red desert dunes alongside brilliant cobalt seas, the dense green of a palm grove in an oasis at the edge of the desert, or the tall skyscrapers that rose from the sand like sculpted, alien life forms?

Or perhaps the people themselves, the shy but welcoming smile of a headscarfed woman, the cheeky grin of tousle-haired boy, pointing at her fair skin and hair?

Marni had no idea. She couldn't give an answer to the question of why she'd fallen in love with this strange, exotic land within hours of stepping off the plane, but in love she was—flushed with excitement as she explored the narrow market lanes that sneaked off the city highways, trembling with delight the first time she dived into the crystal-clear waters, and shyly happy when a group of local women, fellow nurses, asked her to join them for lunch in the hospital canteen.

This was her first day at the hospital, her schedule having allowed her four free days to explore her new home before starting work, and today was more an orientation day, finding her way around the corridors, feeling at home with the unfamiliar layout and the more familiar hospital buzz. Now her new friends were telling her about the theatres where they all worked, which surgeons were quick to anger, which ones talked a lot, which ones liked music as they worked, and which ones flirted.

Hmm! So there *were* some flirts!

Would they flirt with her?

Seriously?

The young women giggled and tittered behind their hands as they discussed this last category and Marni wanted to ask if they flirted back, but felt she was too new to the country and understood too little of the local ways. So she listened to the chat, enjoying it, feeling more and more at home as she realised the women's words could be talk among theatre nurses anywhere in the world, except that it was never personal—no mention of family or relationships—usually the main topics of conversation among nurses back home.

But for all the ease she felt with her fellow nurses, nerves tightened her sinews, and butter- flies danced polkas in her stomach when she re- ported for duty the next day.

'Welcome,' Jawa, one of the nurses she'd met the previous day, said as Marni pushed through the door into the theatre dressing room. 'This morning you will enjoy for Gaz is operating. He's not only a good surgeon, but he takes time to tell us what he is doing so we can learn.'

Aware that many of the staff at the hospital were imports like herself, she wondered if Gaz might be an Australian, the name a shortened Aussie version of Gary or Gareth. Not that she had time to dwell on the thought, for Jawa was handing her pale lavender—lavender?—theatre pyjamas, a cap and mask, talking all the time in her liltingly accented English.

'So we must hurry for he is not one of those surgeons who keep patients or staff waiting. He is always on time.'

Jawa led the way through to the theatre where they scrubbed and gloved up, ready for what lay ahead. The bundle of instruments on the tray at Marni's station—she would be replenishing Jawa's tray as Jawa passed instruments to the surgeon—looked exactly the same as the bundles at home, and relieved by the familiarity of that and her surroundings she relaxed.

Until the gowned, capped, gloved and half-masked figure of the surgeon strode into the room, when every nerve in her body tightened and the hairs on her arms and back of her neck stood to attention.

He's just a man! she told herself, but that didn't stop a tremble in the pit of her stomach as he looked around the room, dark eyes taking in the newcomer, his head nodding in acknowledgement, the eyes holding hers—a second or two, no more—yet causing heat to sear downwards through her body.

'So, we have a stranger in our midst,' the man

who was causing the problems said, his voice reverberating through her like the echoes of carillon bells. 'And you are?'

'Marni Graham, sir,' she said, hoping she sounded more in control than she felt.

'In here I'm Gaz, just Gaz, Marni Graham,' he said. 'Welcome to the team.'

She really should say something—respond in some way—but her voice was lost somewhere in the general muddle of the new and unbelievably vital sensations she was experiencing right now.

Lust at first sight?

It can't be, Marni argued with herself, but silently and very weakly.

The man in question had pulled his mask up to cover his nose and mouth, and seemed about to turn away, but before he did so he smiled at her.

Of course, she couldn't see the smile, not on his lips, but she was certain it was there, shining in his eyes and making her feel warm and very, very unsettled.

What she had to do was to appear totally unaffected by the man, which, of course she was, she told herself. The reaction had been nerves, first day on the job and all that. Yet she was aware of this man in a way she'd never been aware of anyone before, her skin reacting as if tiny invisible wires ran between them so every time he moved they tugged at her.

Was this what had been missing in her other relationships—the ones that had fizzled out, mainly, she had to admit, because she'd backed away from committing physically?

She shook the thought out of her head and concentrated on the task at hand, on the operation, the patient, a child of eight having a second surgery to repair a cleft palate.

'This little boy, Safi, had had his first repair when he'd been six months old,' Gaz was explaining, his voice like thick treacle sliding down Marni's spine. 'That was to repair the palate to help him feed and also to aid the development of his teeth and facial bones.'

He worked as he talked, slender gloved fingers moving skilfully, probing and cutting, everything done with meticulous care, but Marni gave him more points for knowing the child's name and

using it, humanising the patient, rather than calling him 'the child'.

'Now we need to use a bone graft to further
repair the upper jaw where the cleft is, in the
alveolar.'

Marni recited the bones forming part of the
maxilla, or upper jaw bone—zygomatic, frontal,
alveoal and palatine—inside her head, amazed
at what the brain could retain from studies years
ago.

'If we had done this earlier,' Gaz was explaining, 'it would have inhibited the growth of the
maxilla, so we wait until just before the permanent cuspid teeth are ready to erupt before graft-
ing in new bone.'

He continued speaking, so Marni could picture
not only what he was doing but how his work
would help the child who'd had the misfortune
to have been born with this problem.

It had to be the slight hint of an accent in his
words that made his voice so treacly, she decided as he spoke quietly to the anaesthetist. So
he probably wasn't an Australian. Not that it mattered, although some contrary part of her had al-

ready wound a little dream of two compatriots meeting up to talk of home.

Talk?

Ha!

Her mind had already run ahead to the possibility that this man might just be the one with whom she could have that fling.

You're supposed to be concentrating on the job, not thinking about sex!

She hadn't needed the reminder, already shocked by how far her mind had travelled while she'd worked.

And *where* it had travelled!

The man was a complete stranger...

A complete stranger with mesmerising eyes and a sexy, chocolate-syrup voice!

The operation, which seemed to have gone on for ever, wound up swiftly. The surgeon and his assistant left, although Gaz did turn at the door and look around, frowning slightly as he pulled his mask down to dangle beneath his chin, revealing a sculpted line of barely-there beard outlining a jaw that needed nothing to draw attention to its strength.

He nodded in the general direction of the clump of nurses where Marni stood, before disappearing from view.

There was no rush of conversation, which seemed weird as either the surgeons or their skills usually came in for comment during the post-op clean-up. But here the women worked competently and silently, Jawa finally telling Marni that was all they had to do.

'We have time for lunch and you're back in Theatre again this afternoon—you and me both, they have paired us for a while.'

'I'm glad of that,' Marni told her. 'I still need someone to lead me around.'

She opened her mouth to ask if the surgeon called Gaz would be operating again, then closed it, not wanting to draw Jawa's attention to the fact the man had affected her in some strange way.

A *very* strange way!

The afternoon operation was very different, removal of a benign cancer from the ankle of a little girl. The surgeon was French and seemed to think his nationality demanded he flirt with all the nurses, but his work was more than proficient and Marni decided she'd enjoy working here if all the surgeons were as skilled as the first two she'd seen.

A minor operation on a child sent up from ER, repair of a facial tear, finished off her shift, but as she changed into her outdoor clothes she wondered about their first patient, the little boy who'd been born with a deformity that would have been affecting his life. No child liked to look different from his mates...

Uncertain of protocol but needing to know how he'd come out of the operation, Marni asked Jawa if she'd be allowed to see him.

'Just a brief visit to see he's okay,' she added.

Jawa consulted her watch and decided that, yes, he should be well and truly out of Recovery and back on the children's post-op ward.

'Of course you can visit him,' she assured Marni. 'I would come with you but I have an appointment.'

The faint blush that rose in her cheeks as she said this suggested the appointment was special, but Marni forbore to tease, not knowing Jawa or the local customs well enough.

The post-op ward was easy to find. The hospital was set up rather like an octopus with all its tentacles spread flat on the ground. The operating theatres, recovery rooms, the ICU and the administration rooms were all in the tall body of the beast, while the arms supplied different wards.

In the post-op ward, bright with murals of colourful forests and wild animals, Marni found most rooms occupied not only by the patient but by a clutch of family members as well—black-robed women, white-robed men.

'Can I help you?' a passing nurse inquired.

'A little boy who had a cleft palate operation this morning. I was one of the theatre staff and wondered how he was doing.'

'Ah, you mean Safi. Do you wish to visit him?'

'I wouldn't want to intrude on his family,' Marni said.

'You won't,' the nurse told her. 'In fact, it would be good if you could visit him. He's not local but has come here for all his surgery. The hospital takes many children from neighbouring countries because we have the doctors with the skills to help them, and this wonderful facility where they can recover, but often the parents cannot afford to accompany the child. The nurses will do their best to see these children are not too lonely, but most of the time—'

'You're too busy,' Marni finished for her. 'I understand, but I'm far away from home myself so I'll be happy to visit Safi when I can.'

Following the nurse's directions, she found Safi's room, knocked quietly then went in. The little boy turned wide, troubled eyes towards her.

'Hello,' she said, aware he probably had no idea of English but not knowing what language he might speak. 'I've come to visit you.'

She sat beside him and held his hand, wishing she'd brought a toy or a book. Although this boy was eight and she'd been only two when she'd first gone to live with her grandfather, she remembered how Pop had helped her feel at home—he'd sung to her.

Dredging back through her memory, she sang the nursery rhymes of her childhood, using her hands as she had back then, making a star that twinkled in the sky and an itsy-bitsy spider climbing up a water spout.

Safi regarded her quite seriously but when she sang 'Twinkle Twinkle Little Star' for the fourth time, he joined in with his hands then smiled at her.

The smile made her want to cry for his aloneness, but apparently the music had soothed him and he fell asleep.

Not wanting to disturb him too soon, she sat by the bed, holding his hand, her mind drifting through the memories of the tumultuous few weeks since she'd made the decision to come to Ablezia, stumbling out of the drift when she thought of her goal—*her* goal, not Pop's.

Could she do it? Go cold-bloodedly into a relationship with a man simply to rid herself of her virginity?

Hot-bloodedly if it was Gaz! The thought popped into her head and Marni knew heat was colouring her cheeks.

Think sensibly!

It wasn't that she'd thought it precious, the virginity thing. It had just happened, partly, she knew, as the result of having a wayward mother who flitted like a butterfly from man to man.

But the biggest hurdle had been growing up with two elderly men who thought the world of her, and not wanting to ever do anything that would make them think less of her.

So she'd pulled back through her late teens when her friends had been happily, and often unhappily, experimenting with sex, although, to be honest, there'd never been a boy with whom she'd desperately wanted to go to bed.

At university, her lack of experience had embarrassed her enough for her to be cautious, then, probably because of the virginity thing, she'd virtually stopped dating, somehow ashamed to admit, if a relationship *had* developed, her intact state. Until Jack—

Enough brooding!

But Marni still sighed as she lifted the little fingers that had been clasped in hers and kissed the back of Safi's hand.

Who would have thought it could be so hard?

She stole silently out of the room, turning her thoughts back to the child, knowing she'd return and wondering just where she could buy toys and books to cheer the little boy's recovery.

Nelson would send whatever she wanted but he was busy with Pop—she'd check out the internet when she went back to her room.

As she passed the nurses' station, nerves prickled along her spine and glancing over her shoulder she saw the back of a tall, dark-haired man bent slightly to listen to what the nurse at the desk was saying.

Of course it's not him, she told herself, though why had her nerves reacted?

Surely she wasn't going to tingle when she saw every tall, dark and handsome stranger!

CHAPTER TWO

No GAZ IN Theatre the next day or the next, and
Marni decided, as she made her way down the
children's ward to visit Safi, that she was pleased,
she just had to convince herself of the fact. But
the sadness in the little boy's eyes as she entered his room banished all other thoughts. She
sat beside him, took his hand, said 'Hello' then
'*Salaam*', one of the few words she'd managed to
remember from Jawa's language lessons.

Safi smiled and repeated the word, then rattled
off what might have been questions, although
Marni didn't have a clue. Instead she opened up
the folder of pictures she'd printed off the internet, showing Safi a map of Australia and pointing
to herself, then one of Ablezia. Using a cut-out
plane, she showed how she'd flown from Australia to Ablezia.

The little boy took the plane and pointed from

it to her. She nodded. 'Aeroplane,' she said. 'A big jet plane, from here…' she pointed again '…to here.'

Safi nodded but kept hold of the plane, zooming it around in the air.

Marni flipped through her folder, bringing out pictures of a koala, a wombat and a kangaroo. She put them all on the map of Australia and when Safi picked up the picture of the kangaroo, she hopped around the room, delighting the little boy, who giggled at her antics.

'Kangaroo,' she said, hoping the books and toys she'd ordered would arrive shortly—she'd paid for express mail. She'd actually found a female kangaroo with a joey in its pouch among the soft toys for sale, and had made it her number-one priority.

Safi was jumping the picture of the kangaroo on the bed now and pointing towards her, so Marni obligingly jumped again, her hands held up in front of her like the kangaroo's small front paws. Unfortunately, as she spun around to jump back past the end of the bed, she slammed into an obstacle.

A very solid obstacle!

Stumbling to recover her balance, she trod on the obstacle's feet and mashed herself against his chest, burning with mortification as she realised it was the surgeon—Safi's surgeon—the man called Gaz.

'S-s-ir!' She stammered out the word. 'Sorry! Being a kangaroo, you see!'

Marni attempted to disentangle herself from the man.

He grasped her forearms to steady her and she looked up into eyes as dark as night—dark enough to drown in—felt herself drowning...

Fortunately he had enough presence of mind to guide her back to the chair where she'd been sitting earlier and she slumped gratefully into it, boneless knees no longer able to support her weight.

He spoke to Safi, the treacly voice light with humour, making the little boy smile and bounce the picture of the kangaroo around the bed.

'I am explaining to him you come from Australia where these animals are,' Gaz said, turning to smile at her.

The smile finished her demolition. It lit fires she'd never felt before, warming her entire body, melting bits of it in a way she didn't want to consider.

'Well, well, well,' he said, so suggestively she had to wonder if he'd read her reaction to him. Surely not, although the smile playing around his lips—gorgeous lips—and the twinkle in his eyes suggested he might have a fair idea of it.

'You're the new surgical nurse.'

A statement, not a question.

'Marni Graham,' she said, holding out her hand then regretting the automatic gesture as touching him, even in a handshake, was sure to cause more problems.

You've fallen in lust! Twenty-nine years old and you've finally been hit by an emotion as old as time.

'It's not lust,' Marni mumbled, then realised she'd spoken the words, although under her breath so hopefully they hadn't been audible to the surgeon, who was bent over Safi, examining the site of the operation and speaking quietly himself in the soft, musical notes of the local language.

The little boy appeared to know the man quite well, for he was chatting easily, now pointing to Marni and smiling.

'You have visited him before?' Gaz asked as he straightened. 'For any reason?'

'Should I not have come? Is it not allowed?' The man, the questions, her silly reactions all contributed to her blurting out her response. 'Jawa said it would be all right, and the nurses here don't have a lot of time to spend with him.'

The tall man settled himself on the bed, his knees now only inches from Marni's, although she could hardly push her chair back to escape the proximity, tantalising though it was.

They're knees, for heaven's sake!

Marni forced herself to relax.

'Of course you are welcome to visit. Safi appreciates it and looks forward to your visits, but I wondered why you come. You are a stranger here, are you not being looked after? Have you not made friends that you spend your spare time with a child?'

The man had obviously painted her as pathetic.

'Of course I've made friends, and everyone has

been very welcoming, and I've done a lot of exploring, both on my own and with others, but...'

She hesitated.

How to explain that while she loved theatre nursing, the drama of it, the intensity, she missed patient contact?

He was obviously still waiting for an answer, the dark eyes studying her, his head tilted slightly to one side.

'Like most nurses,' she began, still hesitant, 'I took it up because I felt I could offer something in such a career. I enjoyed all the facets of it, but especially nursing children. Early on, I thought I'd specialise in paediatric nursing, but then I did my first stint in Theatre and I knew immediately that's where I really wanted to work. But in Theatre a patient is wheeled in and then wheeled out and somehow, even with the good surgeons who use the patient's name, they don't become real people—there's no follow-up to find out if the operation was a success, there's no person to person contact at all—'

Aware she'd been babbling on for far too long,

she stopped, but when her companion didn't break the silence, she stumbled into an apology.

'Sorry, that sounded like a lecture, sorry.'

He reached out and touched her lightly on the knee, burning her skin through the long, loose trousers she was wearing.

'Do not apologise for showing humanity. It is all too rare a trait in modern medicine where everyone is under pressure to perform and seek perfection in all they do, so much so we have little time to think about those under our care as people rather than patients. In this hospital we allow the families to stay, so our patients have them to turn to, but children like Safi, who have come from a neighbouring country, often have no one.'

'Except you,' Marni pointed out. 'The nurse told me you'd been in earlier and that you stayed with him that first night.'

'I was worried he'd be afraid, alone in a strange place, and I've learned to sleep anywhere so it was no hardship.'

Not only gorgeous but nice, Marni thought, and she smiled at him and told him so—well, not the gorgeous bit.

'That was very kind of you,' she said, 'but have you done it every night? Surely that would be too much if you're operating every day?'

Gaz returned her smile, but it was absent-minded, as if it had slipped onto his lips while he was thinking of something else.

'Not every night, no, but an old friend of mine comes in now and stays with him. It was she who heard the story of a foreign woman visiting.'

'So you came to check?' Marni asked, not sure whether to be pleased or put out. Pleased to have seen him again, that was for sure...

'Of course,' he said. 'Not because I doubted your good intentions, but to see who it was willing to put herself out for a child she did not know.'

The smile this time was the full effort, its effect so electrifying in Marni's body she hoped he'd go away—disappear in a puff of smoke if necessary—so she could sort herself out before she tried standing up.

'And now that I do know,' he continued, oblivious of the effect he was having on her, 'I wondered if you'd like to have dinner with me, a kind of welcome to Ablezia and thank you for being

kind to Safi combined. There is a very good restaurant on the top floor of the administration
building right here in the hospital. We could eat
there.'

So it would seem like colleagues eating together if your wife or girlfriend found about it?
Marni wondered. Or because you have rooms
here and it would be convenient for seduction?
Well, the seduction part would be all right—after
all, wasn't that one of the reasons she was here?

Although annoyed by her totally absurd
thoughts, Marni realised her first question had
been plausible enough—a man this gorgeous was
sure to be taken!

Taking a deep breath, she put the whole ridiculous seduction scenario firmly out of her head.

'I'd like that,' she said, and was surprised to
find her voice sounded remarkably calm. 'That
must be a part of the building I haven't explored
yet. My friend Jawa and I usually go to the staff
canteen on the ground floor.'

Shouldn't you check whether he's married before you get too involved? Marni thought.

Having dinner with a colleague was hardly getting involved!

Or so she told herself!

Until he took her elbow to guide her out of the room.

She knew immediately there was a whole lot wrong with it. She'd made a serious mistake. It was utter madness. That, oh, so casual touch made her flesh heat, her skin tingle and her heart race.

Although wasn't that all good if—

She *had* to stop thinking about seduction!

He dropped her elbow—thankfully—as they walked back up the corridor to the big foyer in the middle of the building, which, again thankfully, gave Marni something to use as conversation.

'It's been beautifully designed, this building,' she said—well, prattled really. 'I love the way this atrium goes all the way up, seemingly right to the roof.

'You'll see the top of some of the taller palms from the restaurant,' Gaz said. 'In arid countries we long for greenery so when there's an opportunity to provide some, either indoors or out, we make the most of it.'

The pride in his voice was unmistakeable and although Marni knew from Jawa that the locals didn't encourage personal conversation, she couldn't help but say, 'So, you're a local, are you?'

The lift arrived and as he ushered her in he smiled at her.

'Very much so.'

The slightly strained smile that accompanied the words told Marni not to pursue the matter, so she talked instead of her delight in the markets, the colours, the people, the aromas.

Still prattling, she knew, but the man made her nervous in ways she'd never been before.

The lift doors slid open, and they stepped out into a glass-sheathed corridor, the inner wall displaying, as Gaz had said, the tops of the palm trees in the atrium.

Drawn to the glass, Marni peered down.

'It's beautiful,' she said, turning to him to share her delight.

He was staring at her, a small frown on his

face, as if something about the sight of her bothered him.

'What?' she asked, and he shook his head, before again, with another light touch on her elbow, guiding her forward, around the atrium to the far side, where a restaurant spread across the corridor so the atrium was indeed visible from the tables.

The place was dimly lit and quiet, only a few tables occupied.

'Are we too early or too late for the usual dinner hour?' Marni asked, desperate to talk about something—anything—to distract herself from the effect this man was having on her, especially with his casual touches and watchful dark eyes.

'Early for the diners coming off late shift, late for those going on night duty,' Gaz told her as the young man on the reception desk greeted Gaz in his own language then bowed them towards a table close to the atrium.

Gaz held up a hand and said something, and the young man bowed again and led them in a new direction so they crossed the room.

'You have seen the tops of the palms in the

atrium,' Gaz explained, 'but possibly not the desert in the moonlight.'

The table was beside a wall of glass, so Marni felt she was seated in space above the long waves of dunes. The moon silvered the slopes it touched, and threw black shadows in between, so the desert seemingly stretched away for ever with a patterned beauty that took her breath away.

'I hadn't known—hadn't realised...'

'That it could be so beautiful?' Gaz asked as her words stumbled to a halt.

She smiled at him, but the smile was an effort because something in the way he said the word 'beautiful' made it seem personal—although that could hardly be true. The women she'd met here were so stunningly attractive she felt like a pale shadow among them, a small daisy among vibrant dark roses.

Answer the man, her head suggested, and she struggled to get back into the conversation—to at least *act* normal in spite of the chaos going on in her body.

'Yes, that,' she said, 'definitely that, but I hadn't realised the hospital was so close to the desert.

I've always come to it from the direction of the city, from the sea side, but the desert's right there—so close you could touch it—and so immense.'

'And dangerous, remember that,' Gaz said.

'Dangerous?' Marni repeated, because once again there seemed to be an underlying message in his words.

It's the accent, you idiot, she told herself. Why should there be some sensual sub-text when the man barely knows you?

'You have deserts in Australia—inhospitable places where a man without water or transport could perish in a few days.'

'Of course. I hadn't thought about it but it would be the same in any desert, I imagine.'

She'd caught up with the conversation, but it hadn't mattered for Gaz was now conferring with a waiter, apparently discussing the menu. He turned to her to ask if she'd like to try some local dishes, and if so, would she prefer meat, fish or vegetarian.

'Meat, please, and yes to local dishes. I've tried some samples of the local cooking in the souks.

There's a delicious dish that seems to be meat, with dates and apricots.'

'And to drink? You would like a glass of wine?'

And have it go straight to my head and confuse me even further?

'No, thank you, just a fruit juice.'

Her voice was strained with the effort of making polite conversation. Her nerves were strung more tightly than the strings of a violin, while questions she couldn't answer tumbled in her head.

Was the attraction she felt mutual?

Could this be the man—not for a lifetime, it was far too early to be considering that—for a fling, an affair?

Worse, could she go through with it if by some remote chance he was interested?

The waiter disappeared and Marni took a deep breath, knowing she somehow had to keep pretending a composure she was far from feeling. But how to start a conversation in a place where personal conversations just didn't seem to happen?

Gaz saved her.

'You mentioned the souks. You have had time to see something of my country?'

She rushed into speech, describing her delight in all she'd seen and done, the beauty she'd discovered all around her, the smiling, helpful people she'd encountered.

Gaz watched her face light up as she spoke, and her hands move through the air as she described a decorated earthen urn she'd seen, or the tiny, multicoloured fish swimming through the coral forests. He saw the sparkle in her pale, grey-blue eyes and the gleam where the lights caught her silvery-blonde hair, and knew this woman could ensnare him.

Actually, he'd known it from the moment he'd seen her—well, seen her pale eyes framed by the white mask and lavender cap on her first day in Theatre.

There'd been something in those eyes—something that had caught at, not his attention but his inner self—a subliminal connection he couldn't put into words.

At the time he'd dismissed the idea as fanciful—the product of a mind overburdened by the changes in his life, but now?

Impossible, of course! He had so much on his plate at the moment he sometimes doubted he'd ever get his head above water.

He groaned inwardly at the mess of clichés and mixed metaphors, but that's how his life seemed right now. He'd stolen tonight from the schedule from hell, and by the time he had his new life sorted, this woman would be gone.

There'll be other women, he reminded himself, then groaned again.

'Are you all right?'

The pale eyes showed genuine concern, and a tiny line of worry creased the creamy skin between her dark eyebrows.

'I will be,' he answered. 'There are some massive changes happening in my life right now, which, as far as I'm concerned, is really bad timing.'

He reached across the table and touched her hand, which was wrapped around the glass of pomegranate and apple juice the waiter had set in front of her.

'Bad timing?' she repeated.

'*Very* bad timing,' he confirmed, and said no more, because he knew that although an attraction as strong as the one he was feeling couldn't possibly be one-sided, there was nothing to be gained from bringing it out into the open. He simply had no time! No time for them to get to know each other properly.

No time to woo her.

Instead, he asked how much diving she'd done, and listened as her quiet, slightly husky voice talked about the Great Barrier Reef, a holiday she'd had in the Seychelles, and compared other dives she'd done with the Ablezian Sea.

Was he listening? Marni had no idea, but she was happy to have something to talk about and as she spoke she relived some of her underwater adventures, and remembering the joy and fun she'd experienced eased the tension in her body so talking now was easy, her companion prompting her to keep going if she lagged.

The meal arrived—a covered earthenware dish set in the middle of the table, another dish of rice set beside it. The waiter added small plates of cut-up salad vegetables and a platter of the flat bread that she was beginning to realise was part of every meal in this country.

'Traditionally, I would serve you, but perhaps you would prefer to help yourself,' Gaz said, lifting the lid of the earthenware pot and releasing the mouth-watering aroma of the dish. 'I would not like to give you too much or too little.'

Ordinary words—common-sense words—so why was she all atingle again?

It was his voice, she decided as she helped herself to rice then added a scoop of the meat dish, before putting a little tomato salad on her plate and taking a piece of bread. His voice sneaked inside her skin and played havoc with her nerves, but when she'd finished her selection and looked across at him, his eyes, intent on her again, caused even more havoc.

Totally distracted now, she picked up her glass of juice and took too big a gulp.

At least half choking to death brought her back to her senses. Marni finished coughing and, flushed with embarrassment, bent her head to tackle her meal.

Fortunately, Gaz seemed to sense her total disarray and took over the conversation, talking about the hospital, built within the last two years, and with the charge of looking after not only local children but those from nearby countries that did not have the facilities this hospital had.

'We have a big oncology department, keeping children here during their treatment so they don't have to travel to and fro. With those children, we try to make sure they have someone from their family travel with them—sometimes, it seems, the entire family.'

His rueful smile at this confession undid all the good concentrating on her food had done for Marni, mainly because it softened his face and somehow turned him from the sexiest man she'd ever laid eyes on to a real, caring human being.

All you're wanting is an affair, not to fall in love, she reminded herself.

But at least hospital talk got them through the meal and when they'd finished, Marni sat back in her chair.

'Thank you, that was utterly delicious. Wonderful. Perhaps I could pay the bill as thanks to you for introducing me to this place? Is that allowed in Ablezia?'

She offered what she knew must be a pathetic smile, but now they'd finished eating she had no idea how to get away—which she needed to do—or what was the polite thing to do next.

Say goodbye and leave?

Wait for him to see her back down to the ground floor?

And if he offered to walk her back to the quarters—through the gardens and lemon orchard, the scented air, the moonlight…

It was too soon even to think about what might happen and the man had already said he had no time.

'You definitely will not pay when I invited you to dinner,' Gaz was saying as she ran these increasingly panicked thoughts through her head. 'It is taken care of but, come, you must see the desert from outside, where you can really appreciate its beauty.'

He rose and came to stand beside her, drawing out her chair, which meant his entire body was far too close to hers when she stood up.

Turning to face him, this time with thanks for the courtesy of the chair thing, brought her even closer—to lips that twitched just slightly with a smile, and eyes that not only reflected the smile but held a glint of laughter.

The wretch knows the effect he's having on me, Marni realised, and found a little anger stirring in the mess of emotions flooding through her body.

Good!

Anger was good—not argumentative anger but something to hold onto. The man was a born flirt and though he obviously couldn't help being the sexiest man alive, he didn't need to use it to snare unwary females.

Wasn't wanting to be snared one of the reasons she'd come here?

Marni ignored the query and allowed Gaz to lead her out of the restaurant and along another corridor that led to a balcony overlooking the desert—the magic sea of black and silver.

She sniffed the air, then breathed it in more deeply.

'It's strange,' she said, turning to her companion, her reaction to him almost forgotten as she

considered the puzzle the desert air presented.
'I know the sea is just over there, but there's no
smell of salt in the air, no smell of the spices escaping from the restaurant or the lemon blossom
that I know is out in the gardens down below us.
No smell at all, really.'

He smiled again—a genuine smile this time,
not a teasing one—but this one made Marni's
heart flutter.

'The desert is a great cleanser. Over the centuries much blood has been spilled on the sands,
and civilisations have risen and collapsed, their
ruins buried by the sand. For people like me,
with Bedouin blood, the desert is as necessary
as water, for it is where we replenish our souls.'

He was serious, the words so graphically beautiful Marni could only shake her head.

And smile.

A small smile but a genuine one.

A smile that for some reason prompted him to
inch a little closer and bend his head, dropping
the lightest of kisses on her parted lips.

Had she started, so that he put his hands on her
shoulders to steady her?

Marni had no idea, too lost in the feel of his lips on hers to think straight.

So when he started talking again, she missed the first bit, catching up as he said, 'You are like a wraith from the stories of my childhood, a beautiful silver-haired, blue-eyed, pale-limbed being sent to tempt men away from their duties.'

She was still catching up when he kissed her again.

Properly this time so she melted against him, parted her lips to his demanding tongue, and kissed him back, setting free all the frustration of the lust infection in that one kiss.

It burned through her body in such unfamiliar ways she knew she'd never been properly kissed before—or maybe had never responded properly—which might explain—

It sent heat spearing downwards, more heat shimmering along her nerves, tightening her stomach but melting her bones.

Her head spun and her senses came alive to the smoothness of his lips, the taste of spice on his tongue, the faint perfume that might be aftershave—even the texture of his shirt, a nubby cotton, pressed against the light cotton tunic top she wore, was sending flaring awareness through her nipples.

A kiss could do all this…

Gaz eased away, shaken that he'd been so lost to propriety as to be kissing this woman, even more shaken by the way she'd reacted to the kiss and the effect it had had on him. Heat, desire, a hardening, thickening, burning need….

For one crazy moment he considered taking things further, dallying with the nurse called Marni, seeing where it went.

Certainly beyond dallying, he knew that much.

Al'ana! Where is your brain? his head demanded. Yes, I thought so! it added as if he'd answered.

He looked at the flushed face in front of him, glimpsed the nipples peaked beneath the fine cotton tunic, the glow of desire in her eyes.

Yes, it would definitely have gone further than dalliance…

'I had no right to do that. I have no time. None! No time at all!' He spoke abruptly—too abruptly—the words harshly urgent because he was denying his desires and angry with himself for—

For kissing her?

No, he couldn't regret that.

Angry at the impossible situation.

This time when he turned to lead her back inside, he didn't touch her elbow and guide her steps but stayed resolutely apart from the seductive siren who'd appeared, not from the sky but in full theatre garb, then jumped like a kangaroo right inside his skin…

Obviously married, Marni told herself. Serves you right, kissing on what wasn't even a first date.

But she was too shaken by the kiss to care what the sensible part of her brain was telling her. Too shaken to think, let alone speak.

Standing silently beside Gaz in the lift, the foot of space between them was more like a million miles.

Back in the foyer, he spoke to one of the young porters who seemed to abound in the place.

'Aziz will see you back to the residence,' Gaz

told her, then he nodded once and was gone, seeming to disappear like the wraith he'd called her.

Aziz was beckoning her towards the door so she followed, deciding she must be right about his marital status if the man she'd kissed didn't want to be seen walking her through the gardens.

So she was well rid of him.

Wasn't she?

Of *course* she was!

The gardens were as beautiful as ever, the scent of lemon blossom heavy in the air, but the magic was dimmed by her memory of the kiss, and now that embarrassment over her reaction was creeping in, she was beginning to worry about the future.

She was a professional. Of course she could work in Theatre with Gaz without revealing how he affected her. Not that he didn't know, given her response, but at least she didn't have to be revealing just how hard and fast she'd fallen for the man.

Lust, her head reminded her, and sadly she agreed.

For all the good it was going to do her when he'd made it obvious he wasn't available!

She sighed into the night air. It was all too complicated!

CHAPTER THREE

HIDING HER REACTIONS to Gaz in Theatre proved unnecessary, because although she worked for five straight days, he was never rostered on in the same theatre as her.

She didn't kid herself that he'd had his schedule changed to avoid her, doubting she was important enough to cause such a change, and caution told her not to mention him to Jawa, not to ask where he was operating or seek answers to any personal questions about the man, in case she unwittingly revealed how she felt.

Besides, they just didn't do personal conversations, these Ablezians.

But her reaction to Gaz had certainly put a damper on her virginity quest, other male colleagues seeming pale and uninteresting by comparison, although she did accept an invitation to the movies from a young doctor on Safi's ward.

She'd even accepted a goodnight kiss but she had felt nothing, not a tingle, not a sign of a spark—and the poor man had known it and had avoided her ever since.

So she worked, visited Safi, and worked again until finally she had time off—three days.

Nelson had emailed to say Pop was talking to the surgeon but was still undecided about the operation, although now he could walk barely a hundred metres without tiring.

She had to forget about Gaz and find a way to see this prince! Once she'd kept her part of the bargain, Pop would *have* to have the operation. He wasn't one to renege on a deal.

And at least sorting out how you're going to approach *him* should get your mind off Gaz, she told herself.

And it did, the whole matter seeming impossible until she read in the English-language newspaper that the new prince had reintroduced his father's custom of meeting with the people once a week. Each Thursday he held court in a courtyard—was that where courtyards got their name?—at the palace, hearing grievances or problems, any subject allowed to approach and speak to him privately for a few minutes.

Reading further, Marni discovered the custom had stopped while his uncle had been the ruler but had been reinstated some weeks previously and was a great success.

She wasn't actually a subject, but that couldn't be helped. If she tied a black headscarf tightly over her hair and borrowed an all-concealing black abaya from Jawa *and* kept her head down— maybe with part of the scarf tied across the lower part of her face—she could slip in with the locals, have a minute to introduce herself and show the photo, perhaps even have a laugh with the man who'd been kind to her as a child.

The planets must have been aligned in her favour—though they'd definitely been against her last week—for the next meeting was the following day.

She emailed Nelson to tell him she was keeping her part of the bargain and to warn Pop she expected him to keep his, then went to collect the clothing she'd need.

Which was all very well in theory!

In practice, once dressed and sitting in the back of a cab on her way to the palace, a building she'd glimpsed from afar in her explorations, she realised just how stupid this was, how ridiculous the whole thing—making a deal with Pop so he'd have a lifesaving operation—fronting up to the prince of a foreign land to show him a photo of himself as a child.

The enormity of it made her shake her head in disbelief.

Yet here she was!

Huge arched gates in a high, sand-coloured wall opened into a courtyard big enough to hold a thousand people. It was an oasis of green— she remembered Gaz telling her how important green was—with beds of flowering roses, tinkling fountains, fruit trees and date palms. The garden had been designed and planted to provide shade but also to form little spaces like outdoor rooms where one could sit and read, or think, or just do nothing.

In the centre, facing the immense, low-set building, was an open grassed area and here the supplicants were gathering, seating themselves cross-legged on the ground in neat rows. Thankfully, there were not as many as Marni had expected, although, contrarily, part of her had hoped there *would* be too many and she could put off her ridiculous venture for another day.

She seated herself beside the last man in the back row, pleased it was a man as she knew he wouldn't attempt to make conversation with a woman he did not know.

An exchange of *salaam*s was enough, Marni with her head bent, not wanting to reveal pale eyes surrounded by even paler skin.

Intent on remaining unseen, she barely heard the words from the wide veranda that ran along the front of the palace. Not that hearing them more clearly would have helped.

Really smart idea, this, she thought despairingly. Just pop along to a meet and greet without a word of the language to tell you when it's your turn to front up to His Maj!

A long line was already forming and as it snaked towards the veranda the man beside her said something then stood and joined the line.

Checking that it already held some women, Marni slid into place behind him, her heart beating such a crazy rhythm she was surprised she could stay upright.

The line inched forward until she could see, on a low couch on the veranda, a white-robed figure, bowing his head as a supplicant approached him, apparently listening to the request or complaint before assigning the person to one of the men who stood behind the couch.

Some people were led to the edge of the veranda and returned to the courtyard, while others were taken in through a door behind the couch, perhaps to sort out business matters or to leave more details. Whatever reason people had to be here, the line moved without a hitch, the meet and greet, as Marni thought of it, a smoothly organised process.

The man in front of her reached the steps, and although instinct told her to flee, the memory of the greyness in Pop's face held her steadfast in the grassy courtyard.

He *had* to have the operation!

The man moved on and one of the flunkeys

supporting the main act waved Marni forward. Following the actions of those she'd seen, she approached swiftly, knelt on the pillow set before the robed figure and bowed her head, then lifted it to look at the face she'd seen in the newspaper back home and on billboards around the city.

The face she'd seen in Theatre, only in his snowy headdress he looked so different...

'But—you're—you're *you*,' she managed to get out before words evaporated from her head.

Gaz was staring at her, as bemused as she was apparently, although once again she suspected there was a smile hovering somewhere in his eyes.

'I am,' he finally said. 'Definitely me. How may I help you?'

The voice had its usual effect, and Marni dissolved completely into a morass of words and half-sentences that she knew were making no sense at all.

'Stupid, I knew that—but Pop needs the op—and then the photo—photos really—you were in the paper—and the job there—here—and I know it's silly but he really wanted—so I came—'

'You came?' Gaz repeated.

Marni took a deep breath, looked into the face of the man she lusted after and smiled at the absurdity of it all.

'Actually,' she said, almost totally together now, 'I came to—well, to say hello and show you a photo. Apparently we were betrothed, you see, a long time ago, and I know it's stupid but I promised Pop I'd try to meet you and—'

She was rattling on again so she stopped the babble and reached into the pocket of her borrowed abaya, but before she could pull out the photo the man she'd written off as a flunkey had grabbed her wrist in a grip of steel.

'I think she wants to marry me, not shoot me,' Gaz said, adding something in his own language so the man withdrew his hand and stepped away, leaving Marni burning with embarrassment.

Gaz took the photo, frowning at it, thinking back perhaps, looking from it to Marni, shaking his head, serious now, although a gleam of amusement shone deep in his eyes.

'Oh, but this is wonderful!' he finally declared, a delighted smile flashing across his face. 'We cannot talk now, but you have no idea how fortuitous this is. Mazur will take you to a side room, get you tea or a cold drink. I will join you shortly.'

Marni was still trying to work out the wonderful and fortuitous bits when Gaz reached out to help her back to her feet, indicating she should follow the man who'd stepped forward on his other side.

Totally bewildered by the whole charade—Gaz was Prince Ghazi? How could that be?—she followed Mazur, stumbling slightly as she was about to enter the room and realising she hadn't removed her sandals.

They entered a huge, open room, with high, arched doorways curtained in what looked like gold-coloured silk, the drapes pulled back and held with golden, heavily tasselled cords. The floor was of white marble, inlaid with coloured stones that made twining patterns of leaves and flowers, so brilliantly beautiful she had to pause to take them in.

Scattered here and there were immense carpets, woven in patterns of red, blue and green. Low settees were placed at intervals along the walls, cushions piled on them. Here and there, groups of people sat or stood, obviously waiting for further conversation with Gaz—Prince Ghazi!

'This is the *majlis*, the public meeting room,' Mazur explained. 'but you will be more comfortable in a side room.' He led her towards an arched opening to one side of the big area and into a smaller version of it—patterned marble floor, a bright rug and a pale yellow sofa with bright cushions scattered over it.

Mazur waited until she was seated on the softly sprung sofa before asking, 'You would like tea perhaps? We have English tea or mint tea, cardamom, of course, and other flavours if you wish.'

His English was so impeccable, his courtesy so effortless he could have worked for English royalty.

Though apparently Gaz *was* royalty...

And she'd *kissed* him? Considered—well, more than considered—him a potential lover!

'Mint tea would be lovely,' Marni managed to reply, and waited until he'd departed before burying her head in her hands, desperate to make sense of what had happened.

She was finishing her tea and nibbling on one of the little cakes Mazur had produced when Gaz appeared, looking so utterly regal in his pristine white robe and starched headdress, a coronet of black silk cord holding it in place, that her heart fluttered again but this time with a degree of not fear but definitely trepidation.

'So, we are betrothed?' he teased, not bothering to hide his smile.

'Well, that's what Pop wrote, but who knows what your father put underneath—probably something about pleasing a daft old man—but it was all just a kind of a joke, me coming here. I didn't come here to hold you to a ridiculous betrothal, but with Pop so sick I made a deal with him. It's hard to explain...'

Marni was doing her best to sort things out, but she was becoming increasingly annoyed because the wretched man was so obviously amused by the whole thing while she was squirming with embarrassment.

Gaz came closer and the white gown did nothing to stop all the physical manifestations of lust that had struck Marni when she'd first set eyes on him.

Lust, she had discovered very quickly, was stronger than embarrassment, for all the good it was going to do her. This man was way out of her league in every way, so a casual affair was out of the question.

She watched him, nervous, apprehensive, wondering just what he might be thinking.

'Actually,' he said, coming to sit beside her on the couch, 'the betrothal is a splendid idea. You may not know it but I have seven sisters, six of whom are bent on finding me a wife.'

'Only six?'

Marni was interested in spite of herself, although she had to admit to a little twinge of dread as to where this betrothal idea might be leading.

'The seventh's heavily pregnant at the moment and fortunately has other things on her mind. But having six sisters producing eligible women for you almost daily is very difficult, especially when I'm trying to come to terms with this job. So your arrival has come at just the right time, and with the photo as proof that my father arranged it, my sisters can do nothing but accept it. It's perfect!'

Marni stared at him in disbelief.

'Perfect?'

'Absolutely perfect!' The dark eyes were definitely smiling.

'Are you saying you'll tell your sisters we're betrothed?'

'Of course.'

She shook her head then pulled herself together enough to demand, 'But that's all? Just betrothed? A temporary arrangement to stop them dangling women in front of you? That's all you want?'

'For the moment,' the white-robed figure replied, while Marni quelled an urge to run a fingertip along the fine dark line of his beard. 'I wouldn't rush you into marriage.'

'Marriage!'

The word came out as a startled squeak, and it was the squeak that brought her to her senses.

Mature, professional women did not squeak!

'Let's just back up here,' she said firmly, trying hard not to notice how exotically handsome he looked in his prince outfit. 'I know it was a ridiculous thing for me to do, coming here and rattling on about a betrothal, but you were meant—no, you weren't meant to be you to start off with— you were meant to be this kindly prince and I'd burble out my stuff, you'd laugh, I'd let Pop know I'd done it, he'd have the op to keep his part of the bargain, and everything would be fine.'

She hesitated then added, 'To be honest, it did cross my mind you might not be so kindly and I just might end up in a dungeon or deported at the very least, but Pop needed—'

Gaz held up his hand, the white robe falling back from his lower arm so Marni could see his wrist, fine dark hairs on his forearm, smooth olive skin...

'This Pop you talk of—he's the one who wrote on the photo?'

Marni swallowed hard, unable to believe a little bit of a man's arm could have excited her so much.

She managed a nod.

'What operation?'

Whether it was the tension of the day or her concern over Pop or simply relief to be talking about something other than her reason for being here, suddenly words flowed freely.

How Pop had always been an active man, involved in so many things, running different charities, on the boards of hospitals and refuges, years ago two stents had been put in and he'd continued on without missing a beat then suddenly this tiredness, exhaustion and a diagnosis of a faulty heart valve and blocked stents, two bypasses and open-heart surgery the only answer.

'We're sure he'll get through it, Nelson and I, but Pop feels at his age maybe it isn't worth it—'

Again Gaz lifted his hand and this time Marni refused to look at that erotic bit of forearm.

'Nelson?' Gaz asked, frowning now.

'The man who looks after Pop—he's been there for ever, looked after me as well. A kind of general factotum.'

But Gaz wasn't listening. He'd pulled out the photo and was staring at it.

'Where was this taken?' he demanded, and Marni explained.

'Apparently your father took over the whole hotel,' she added, and Gaz smiled.

'He was never one to do things by halves and I suppose if I was as young as I look then some of my sisters would already have been married, then there were the wives and the aunts and all the women the women needed to look after them whenever they travelled. But if he took over the whole hotel, where did you come into it?'

So Marni explained about the apartments.

'Pop bought one when the hotel was built and still lives there with Nelson, so when I was dumped on him by my mother, I lived there too. We were allowed to use all the hotel facilities so I probably met you in the pool or garden.'

'Nelson!' Gaz said. 'That's what brought it back to me. I kept calling him Mr Nelson and he'd tell me, no, his name was Nelson.'

He looked from the picture to Marni then back to the picture, tracing his finger across the images of the two children.

'I asked you to marry me,' he said quietly.

Being flabbergasted took a moment, then Marni laughed.

And laughed!

'Oh,' she said, finally controlling her mirth,

'that's what it must be about. A child's proposal—
the sort of thing that would happen at kindergar-
ten—then your father and Pop humouring you by
having the photo taken and writing on the back.'

It took her a moment to realise her amusement
wasn't shared. In fact, Gaz was looking particu-
larly serious.

'But don't you see?' she said. 'It was a joke between the two men. It's not as if it meant anything.'

Gaz continued to study her.

'Would you mind very much?' he asked after
the silence had stretched for ever.

'Mind what?'

'Being betrothed to me?'

Mind? Marni's heart yelled, apparently very
excited by the prospect.

Marni ignored it and tried to think, not easy
when Gaz was sitting so close to her and her
body was alive with its lustful reactions.

'To help you out?' she asked, hoping words
might make things clearer. 'With your sisters?'

Gaz smiled, which didn't help the lustful business and all but destroyed the bit of composure she'd managed to dredge up.

'That, of course, but it's more than the sisters. I have to explain, but perhaps not here, and definitely not now. There are people I need to see, supplicants from this morning. Are you free for the rest of the day? Would you mind very much waiting until I finish my business? Mazur will see you are looked after, get you anything you want. You could explore the garden or even wander around the palace. It's exceptionally empty now without the harem, so you needn't worry about disturbing anyone.'

He touched her hand and stood up, apparently taking her compliance for granted, although, in fact, her mind had stopped following the conversation back when he'd said the word 'harem', immediately conjuring up visions of dancing girls in see-through trousers and sequinned tops, lounging by a pool or practising their belly dancing. Was it because he'd said the word with a long 'e' in the last syllable, making 'hareem' sound incredibly erotic, that the images danced in her head?

She watched the white-clad back disappear through a side door.

He *had* made it sound as if the lack of a harem was a temporary thing, a slight glitch, she reminded herself. Which meant what?

And wasn't having no harem a positive thing?

What was she thinking?

A harem or lack of one would only affect her if she was *really* betrothed to him, and as far as she could remember—it had been a very confusing conversation—she hadn't actually agreed to even a pretend betrothal.

Had she?

And surely harems no longer existed?

Not dancing-girl harems anyway...

She pushed herself off the sofa and, too afraid to wander through the palace, even one without a 'hareem', she retreated to the gardens, thinking of pronunciations. Gaz with its short 'a' sound, suggested a friendly kind of bloke, sexy as all hell but still the kind of man with whom one might have had an affair, while Ghazi—which she'd heard pronounced everywhere with a long 'a', like the one in 'bath', sounded *very* regal.

Frighteningly regal!

And it totally knocked any thought of using the man to overcome her other problem right on the head! Ordinary women like Marni Graham of Australia didn't go around having affairs with kings or princes.

Even a pretend betrothal was mind-boggling!

A wide path led to a central fountain and, after playing with the water for a while, she turned onto another path, this one running parallel to the main building, leading to what appeared to be another very large building. In front of it, on a wide lawn, four boys were kicking a soccer ball. A wayward kick sent the ball hurtling in her direction and, mindful of Nelson's coaching tips, she kicked it back, high and hard, aiming it at the tallest of the boys, who raced to meet it and headed it expertly towards the makeshift goal—two small topiary trees spaced conveniently apart.

The lad high-fived all round then turned towards her, speaking quickly.

Marni held up her hand and shook her head.

'I'm sorry, I don't understand your language.'

The older boy came closer, looking her up and

down, waving his hands towards her clothing as if to ask why she was dressed like she was.

She lifted up the black abaya to show her jeans and the boys laughed, the tall one inviting her to join the game.

'That's if you can run in a skirt?' His easy command of English made her wonder if he went to school overseas, or perhaps to an English language school here.

'I'm sure I can,' she assured him, and joined the boys, kicking the ball from one end of the grassed area to the other. She'd just sent it flying over the top of the topiary goal posts when a tall figure appeared, not in scrubs, or in the intimidating white gown, but in jeans as faded as hers, and a dark blue polo shirt that had also seen better days.

'Ghazi!' the boys chorused in delight. 'Come and play. This is Marni, she's nearly as good as you.'

Although he'd been looking for her, he'd hardly expected to find her playing soccer with his young nephews. The hood of her cloak had slipped off her head and her headscarf was dangling down the back of her neck, hiding the thick plait of fair hair. Her face was flushed, but whether from exertion or embarrassment he had no idea, and she was the most beautiful thing he'd ever seen.

Best not to get further entangled, his common sense warned, for all the betrothal idea was so appealing. But against all common sense he joined the game for a few minutes then told the boys he had to take their playmate away.

He was pleased to see they all went up to her and held out their hands to say goodbye, only Karim, the eldest, bold enough to invite her to play with them again.

How old was Karim? Surely not yet a teenager, although these days who knew when hormonal changes would rear their heads.

Marni had fixed her scarf and pulled the hood back over her head as she approached him.

'I do hope I wasn't doing the wrong thing,' she said, the flush still visible in her cheeks. 'The ball came towards me, I kicked it, and next thing I knew I was part of the game. They're good, the boys. I played for years myself, never good enough to make a rep team but enough to know skill when I see it.'

'They're soccer mad, just as their father is. His dream is to get Ablezia into the World Cup. For a country that doesn't yet have its own international team, it's a huge task. I'm pretty sure that's why I landed this job.'

'This job?'

The pale grey-blue eyes looked into his, the question mirrored in them.

'Ruler—supreme commander—there are about a dozen titles that my major-domo reads out on formal occasions. My uncle succeeded my father, who was an old man when I was born—the first son after seven daughters. Here, our successors are chosen from within the family but not necessarily in any particular order, but I had assumed Nimr, my cousin, would succeed *his* father and I could continue my surgical work, but Nimr the Tiger didn't want the job—his focus is on sport—and so here I am.'

Had he sounded gloomy that he felt soft fingers touch his arm?

'Is it such a trial?' the abaya-clad blonde asked.

'Right at this very moment?' he asked, covering her hand with his. 'Not really!'

The boys started whistling as boys anywhere in the world would do at the tiniest hint of romance, and he stepped back, gave them what he hoped was a very princely glare and put his hand on Marni's back to guide her away from them.

He'd have liked to tell them to keep quiet about her, but that would only pique their curiosity further, and he knew that before they'd even eaten lunch the boys would have relayed the story of the soccer-playing visitor to Alima, his eldest sister, wife of Nimr and mother of the precious boys they'd waited so long for.

'And the prime mover in the "find a wife" campaign,' he added, the words spoken aloud before he realised it.

'Who's the prime mover?' Marni asked, stopping by a pomegranate tree and fiddling with her scarf.

Gaz explained the relationship.

'Is that why they live so close? Not in the main building but within the walls?'

He looked at her, wondering if the question

was nothing more than idle curiosity, although he was coming to believe that was unlikely. He was coming to see her as a woman who was interested in the world around her, eager to learn about it and discover new things.

Could this crazy idea work beyond a pretend betrothal?

'My uncle was living in the palace when they married, so naturally he built them the house nearby. This palace is new, or newish. My father built it when he tired of travelling from our home in the old city to here. Ablezia came late into the modern world, and we are a people who are slow to change. Obviously when the world changed so dramatically in these parts, we *had* to change— to learn new ways, to understand the intricacies of new business structures and international relations. My father was the right man for the job, because he understood it had to happen.'

'And you?' his perhaps betrothed asked softly. 'Are you the right man for the job?'

CHAPTER FOUR

GAZ—SHE COULDN'T think of him as anything else—didn't reply, simply putting one hand in the small of her back to guide her along a path between the huge houses towards what looked like stables beyond more garden.

Not stables but garages.

'There *are* horses,' he said, 'at the old palace, but I think my father realised we'd have no use for them here, so where, traditionally, the stables would be, he built "stalls" for cars.'

'So many cars?' Marni queried, seeing the long line of garages.

Gaz shrugged.

'Oh, you never know when someone might need to go somewhere,' he said, nodding to an elderly man who came forward to meet them. The man wore the loose trousers and long tunic top common among the locals, with a snug-fitting, embroidered cap on his head.

Listening to the fluid sounds of the words as Gaz spoke, Marni felt a longing to learn the language—to learn all she could about this fascinating country, although, she realised rather glumly, once the pretend betrothal ended she'd certainly have to leave.

If there *was* a pretend betrothal…

'I was explaining we won't need a big car and driver, but Fayyad is horrified. He feels I'm not respecting my position enough.'

Again a touch on the small of her back, and her body's inevitable response.

Gaz steered her to where a battered four-wheel drive was relegated to a car port rather than a garage, and held the passenger door open for her.

Still totally bemused by the outcome of this visit to the palace, Marni climbed in. The day had taken on a dream-like quality, and she was moving through the dream without conscious thought. Gaz slid in behind the wheel and drove out through a rear gate, waving to the two men who squatted on the ground beside the big open doors.

'To answer your question,' Gaz said, taking what seemed like a little-used track that appeared to lead directly into the desert, 'I am reluctantly coming to the conclusion that I *am* the right man for the job, although I would far rather have continued my surgical career. All I can hope is that once I've got the job sorted—I've only been in it a couple of months—I can continue operating, at least on a part-time basis.'

Intrigued by his answer, Marni turned to look at him—not a good idea, for he flashed her a smile and the reactions the light touch on her back had stirred came fully to life.

'So, what's the job, as we seem to be calling it, entail?'

Another flashing smile, though this one was slightly rueful.

'I'm still coming to grips with it, but it's mostly formal stuff—meeting representatives from foreign countries, listening to delegations from various committees, making rulings on things that are more to do with our cultural heritage than politics—we have an elected congress that takes care of politics. And then there's the entertaining—endless entertaining.'

The road had petered out and he drove swiftly and skilfully across the sand, taking a slanting line across a dune and pulling up on the top of it. Beneath them the sand fell away to rise again, and again, and again, rolling waves of red-gold, brilliant in the sunshine. Breathtaking in its beauty. Marni remembered what he'd said about the desert being as necessary as water to his people. Did he need its power now? Need to refresh himself in the same way as she looked to the ocean for the replenishment of her spirit?

She was staring at the dunes, her mind asking questions she couldn't answer, so didn't realise he'd climbed out of the car and walked around to open her door. Beyond him, she could see a low-slung shelter, dark cloth of some kind, held up in front by sturdy poles, high enough to sit under to escape the sun. In front of it a low fire burned, beside the fire were two ornate silver coffee-pots, like others she'd seen in the souk.

'Come,' he said. 'We have to eat so why not here?'

He took her hand to help her down, his words

perhaps answering her question about his need for the power of the desert.

Leading her to the shelter, he motioned to a faded rug, spread on the sand and heaped with cushions. A large woven basket was set in the shade beside the rug, its lid open to reveal an array of goodies.

Marni sank onto the rug, tucking her legs sideways so the abaya fell around her. The desert was framed now by the dark material of the tent and she could only shake her head in the wonder of its beauty.

Shake her head about the fact that she was actually here, not to mention seeing it with the man who ruled the country.

Impossible!

Gaz settled beside her, closer to the fire.

'We must have coffee first,' he said, lifting one of the ornate pots and taking two tiny handle-less cups from the top of the basket. He poured the strong, thick brew easily into the tiny cups, passing her one before setting the pot back by the fire.

'Traditionally you should drink three cups, but

it's definitely an acquired taste so you may stop at one.'

His smile teased at her senses and in an attempt to settle herself she gulped the drink, tasting the gritty lees but not finding them distasteful.

'And now we eat,' he said, and she wanted to protest—to ask what they were doing there, apart from picnicking, of course. To question the betrothal stuff and try to sort out what was happening. But he was producing bread, and cold meats, salad vegetables and fruit, serving her this time, piling goodies on a silver platter, handing it to her and urging her to eat.

Looking at the food, varied and enticing, she realised how hungry she was, and, not having much option now he'd handed her the plate, she ate.

Gaz watched her while he ate, wondering about this woman fate had thrust into his life. She was using her bread as cutlery, in the local way, and managing to do it without too much spillage. And as she ate she smiled, or muttered little sounds of appreciation, looking up from time to time to ask what a particular morsel might be.

She fascinated him, and not just in a physical way, although the physical attraction was extremely strong. Could this extraordinary idea work?

It was certainly worth a try.

He thought back to the night he'd first kissed her on the balcony outside the restaurant and remembered the surge of desire he'd felt—a surge that had almost led to his suggesting they take it further...

A betrothal would put that off limits. He could hardly be seen sneaking in and out of her room, or sneaking her in and out of the palace, although...

There was no although, but what if the betrothal led to marriage?

It needn't be a long betrothal, and if the marriage didn't work he would make sure she was amply compensated—these things were understood in his country...

Marriage was the logical answer. His body tightened at the thought, but she hadn't actually said yes to the betrothal, had she? He'd have to start there, he realised as she set aside her plate, all but empty, and wiped the damp, scented towel he handed her, across her lips.

'That was amazing,' Marni told him as she put her plate down on another mat. 'Just amazing!'

He turned to her, and reached out to touch her chin, tilting her head so he could look into her face.

'I'm glad,' he said, 'and now we're both fed, perhaps we can get back to the conversation.'

'The job?'

'The job!' he confirmed. 'Actually, endless entertaining is more time-consuming than difficult. I'm concerned that it might bore you to death.'

He had moved towards her as he spoke and now he leant forward and kissed her on the lips.

Thankfully, the shock of what he'd said lingered long enough to prevent Marni from responding to the kiss.

'Won't bore *me* to death?' she shrieked. 'Why on earth would it bore *me* to death?'

Now he frowned, and his eyes seemed darker than ever, though could black be any blacker?

'You think you'd enjoy it?' he asked. and it was her turn to frown.

'Why should I enjoy it, or be bored by it?' she demanded.

His answer was a smile, and if she'd managed to squelch her reaction to the kiss, she failed with the smile.

'Because, as my betrothed, you'll be by my side a lot of the time. I know that's an imposition, but I have women who'll help you all the way. The harem will be back in the palace next week, and I've sisters and nieces and cousins, even aunts, who'll be only too happy to shop with you for suitable clothes, to set you up with anything you need, and make sure you know the protocols.'

It would have been confusing if once again Marni's mind hadn't balked at the 'harem' word. Although if it was only a pretend betrothal, did the harem really matter?

Yes!

'This harem?' she asked, then stopped as she really didn't think she could mention belly-dancing females in see-through trousers.

'The harem?' Gaz repeated, making it exotic again with his pronunciation.

He looked puzzled then suddenly began to chuckle.

'You weren't imagining a seraglio, where you?'

'I've no idea what a seraglio is,' Marni said crossly, 'but if it's scantily clad women, lounging around limpid pools eating grapes and belly dancing then, yes—that's how everyone *I* know imagines a harem.'

The chuckle became a laugh and looking at him, with the tension she'd seen earlier washed from his face, she was once again tugged into the extraordinary sensual power of this man.

'The harem is simply a group name for the women of the family—women and children, in fact. My mother is part of it, my father's other wives, aunts and cousins and even more distant relations, also friends of all the women. Some come and go but the core of them moves together.

'Right now they are all at the old palace where one of my nieces is preparing her wedding chest. Years ago it would have meant a trip to London and Paris and taking over hotels, having stores like Harrods opening at night especially for them, but now they've discovered the internet, shopping has taken on a whole new dimension.'

There was more than a touch of cynicism in his voice so it took a moment for Marni to absorb what he'd said—taking over an entire store?—and then she wondered about the wedding chest. Should she ask? No, another diversion would take her further from where she needed to be.

'Okay,' she began then found she didn't know how to continue. She gazed out at the desert sands but there was no help to be had there. *What* had he been saying before she was thrown off track?

Shopping, suitable clothes, protocol—

'Okay?' Gaz prompted gently, and she turned to face him once again, his gentle smile causing so much confusion she stuttered into speech.

'B-b-but if it's just pretend—just for your sisters—do I have to do all that formal stuff? The "by your side" stuff? I've got my job, you know—well, of course you do—so surely...'

The words fell off her lips as something in his eyes—intensity, or was it intent?—caused such severe palpitations in her chest she couldn't breathe.

It had been intent she'd read. She realised that the moment his lips, once again, closed on hers.

Her mind shut down completely.

Was it a minute or an hour later that he released her? She had no idea, only knew she felt so weak and shaken she had to lean against him, her breath coming in little gasps, her brain slowly returning to work, though not offering much by way of explanation as to why this man, of all the men she'd met in her life, should have such a disastrous effect on her.

Nothing to do with the fact he's the most gorgeous guy in the known universe, the voice in her head suggested.

There was that, of course, but why her?

He eased away, smiling at her, a teasing smile, as if he knew exactly how much damage his kisses did to her.

'I don't think we have to pretend about the attraction between us,' he murmured, and the shiver that ran down Marni's spine told her just how dangerous this situation was.

'But that's different. It's the betrothal thing—*that's* the pretence.'

She was babbling again!

'So you're not denying the attraction?'

The words may have been innocent but she heard the challenge behind them and glared at him.

Pulling herself together with a mammoth effort, she tried again.

'I'm not talking about the attraction, Gaz,' she began, then hoped she wasn't breaking some unknown protocol by continuing to call him that. 'I know I started this nonsense about the betrothal by showing you the picture and, yes, when you said it would help you out, I kind of went along with it. But appearing in public, wearing clothes, meeting people, deceiving them really, well, I don't think that's quite me.'

'You'd rather meet people naked?'

It was the glint in his eyes as much as the words that made her want to belt him one. Except she probably *would* be thrown into a dungeon if she hit the ruling prince.

Would that be such a bad idea? A nice cool jail cell with no diversions?

'You know what I mean,' she retorted. 'It's not

so much the fuss and public stuff, though that's mind-boggling enough, but the—the deception. I mean, your family, your mother, people who care about you, what are they going to think when the pretence ends and I go back home?'

He smiled and took her hand, rubbing his thumb across the backs of her fingers, sending tingling messages along her nerves and searing heat through her body.

'Don't worry about that for an instant—they'll all blame me. I've been a lost cause to the family ever since I insisted on studying medicine instead of business or commerce. It's one of the reasons I thought I was safe from the ruler's job, but as it turned out, there are so many people in our parliament and public service with all the right degrees, the fact that I don't have a huge amount of knowledge about international business isn't a disadvantage.'

Somehow his mood had changed and Marni sensed hidden depths in this man, for all he joked about the 'job'.

'But you *do* know people, surely that's more

important than a business degree,' she said softly, and his hand tightened on her fingers.

'Ah!' he said softly. 'So someone understands.'

Uncertain what he meant, Marnie was about to ask, but he'd turned to look out at the desert again, and she sensed a remoteness in him, as if he was disconnected by his thoughts.

Disconnected from her as well.

Did someone not want him to be the ruler?

Someone in his family?

Or did he feel detached from his family?

Had it been a real problem for him, going against their wishes to follow his own path? He had certainly seized on her silly betrothal photo, grabbing it like a drowning man would grab a tiny stick, so his sisters' representations must have been bothering him.

And now you're back at the betrothal!

Had he guessed that her thoughts had returned to it that he turned back to her and lifted his hand to tuck a stray lock of hair behind her ear?

'Maybe our betrothal could turn out to be more than a pretence, Marni,' he suggested, his voice deep and husky.

With desire?

She was still wondering when he continued, 'We may not know each other very well, but there's time enough to remedy that, and you can't deny the attraction between us.'

His eyes held hers.

No, she couldn't deny the attraction, but...

She shook her head.

'I'm sorry, but I simply cannot imagine what would lie ahead, so how could I possibly agree to anything?'

'I would be there with you all the way. I would give you every support, give you anything you needed or wanted,' he said, his voice so serious she found herself shivering, although the air was warm.

The tension in the shade of the tent was palpable now, so thick Marni imagined she could feel it pressing against her skin and taste it on her lips.

But how to break it?

'Let's just go with the betrothal for now,' she said. 'And maybe keep it quiet—just letting your sisters—your family—know. You can use the excuse of Pop's operation—blame me for not wanting a fuss at this stage. Then if you need me to accompany you to official functions, I can start slowly, so it isn't some big deal but something people gradually get used to. Would that be possible?'

He rested his palm against her cheek.

'Anything is possible,' he said, as he slid the hand behind her head to draw her close.

The kiss was so gentle she responded in spite of herself.

Responded and was lost.

Admittedly, with Pop and Nelson's opinion of her always in her mind, she'd come late to the kissing scene, although she'd eventually made up for lost time, exchanging kisses with any number of young and not so young men over the years.

But had she ever experienced a kiss that made her toes tingle?

A kiss that sent shivers spiralling along her nerves, sensitising the skin at the back of her neck, along her arms, across her breasts, not to mention other places previously immune to spiralling shivers?

Not that she could recall.

And surely if she had, she wouldn't have the other problem.

Dear heaven, she was melting, disintegrating, a helpless mass of quivering flesh.

His hand was moving on her arm, leaving lines of heat where it had touched yet still his lips held her in thrall, held her and seduced her, his searching tongue making promises she barely understood.

Eventually he lifted his head, looking down into what was undoubtedly a face flushed scarlet by her reactions.

'I'll need to find you somewhere to live,' he said as calmly as if he hadn't just destroyed any common sense and will-power she might once have had. 'The harem would swamp you, drive you mad with all their so-called help. My sister, Tasnim, the pregnant one, would be best. Her husband is away so she'll enjoy the company. She's banished all the women in her family to the main harem because they were fussing over her too much, but she'll love to have you visit.'

Still trying to collect herself post-kiss, Marni could only stare at him. Then, as the words took on a slightly suggestive air, she pulled herself together.

'I have a perfectly good little flat at the hospital,' she reminded him.

He smiled in such a way the shivers started all over again, but rather than pointing out that he couldn't be seen visiting her at the nurses' quarters, he merely said, 'Security!' and helped her up off the mat, leading her back to the car, seeing she was buckled in.

Was he really intending to go through with this absurd betrothal? Gaz asked himself as he eased the vehicle back down the dune.

He thought of the kiss and the fires it had lit within him, then shook his head at the absurdity of the situation.

Was it lust or simply one-upmanship against his sisters that was making him push it?

And if it was lust, wasn't becoming betrothed to her the one certain way of ensuring he couldn't act on the lust—well, not beyond a few very heated kisses?

Very, *very* heated kisses, he amended, thinking

of the taste of her, the softness of her lower lip as he'd sucked it gently into his mouth...

He glanced at the woman who sat so quietly beside him, the colour subsiding from her cheeks. If he could only get past his visions of how good they'd be in bed, maybe he could think clearly about the future—the immediate future anyway.

Men in his family didn't marry for sex. Such appetites could be satisfied in other ways with willing partners who were well looked after financially when the arrangement ended.

Not that he'd had any such arrangements, though there'd been affairs, some almost serious, during his student and university days.

But marriage?

Essentially, one married to produce children, but also, more often than not, for political reasons—uniting warring tribes, gaining power against a neighbour, improving the bloodlines of their breeding horses or camels.

He found himself chuckling at the thought and when the blonde who'd exploded into his life turned towards him, he shared his thoughts—not the children part, but the rest.

She grinned at him.

'Well, if your camels need some improvement in their genetic make-up then even being betrothed to me might ruin your chances with someone whose father has vastly superior camels.'

He reached out to touch the silvery fair hair.

'My camels will just have to take their chances, although you have no idea what a sacrifice I'll be making. My family have bred beautiful camels for generations. And we expect to win most of the prizes at the annual camel show.'

'A camel show? The camels all on show? How are they judged?'

Her interest was so apparent he felt warmth stirring inside him—something quite different from the heat he'd experienced earlier. This was pleasure, pure and simple—pleasure at how this woman took such an interest in everything about his country, a genuine interest that went beyond politeness. He wanted to stop and talk to her again, this time about the camels—*his* camels—but the palace was in sight and he'd already stolen too much time out of his schedule.

He slowed the car then stopped so he could explain.

'I must go back to my office before someone sends out a search party, but Fayyad will drive you to the hospital and wait while you pack, then take you to Tasnim's house. Fayyad will let me know when you are on your way and I will meet you there. In the meantime, I will phone her and explain and organise a permanent driver for you if you want to continue to work while we make the necessary arrangements for our betrothal.'

He saw the objections rising in her mind but before she could launch them he claimed her lips once again, thankful for the darkly tinted windows in the vehicle for they were right outside the palace gates.

He felt her resistance, but only momentarily…

CHAPTER FIVE

MARNI SANK DEEP into the softly cushioned seats in the black limousine and battled to make sense of the day. Not even a full day, for it was still early afternoon. Yet here she was being driven to her flat under orders to pack and go off to stay with a total stranger—a pregnant stranger—who would help her deal with being betrothed to the country's ruler.

How had this happened to her?

She certainly hadn't set out to become betrothed to the man—all she'd wanted was for Pop to have his operation.

Pop!

What on earth could she tell Pop?

She heard the groan that escaped her lips then realised she needn't tell him anything—not yet. All she had to do was email to say she'd kept her part of the bargain and met Ghazi, and she expected Pop to let her know the date of his operation.

Ghazi!

The Gaz-Ghazi thing was a whole different problem. Yes, she'd been attracted to Gaz right from the beginning, but the man she'd been kissing wasn't Gaz, he was Prince Ghazi and given that the betrothal was a pretence, she really should stop responding to his—Gaz's? Ghazi's?—kisses.

Shouldn't she?

Nothing was going to come of it—of the kissing business. Given her private reason for coming to Ablezia, she might well have had an affair with Gaz if things had turned out differently, like if he'd been Gary from Australia, but she had a nasty suspicion that rulers of places like this didn't have affairs with women to whom they were publicly betrothed. With other women probably, but not their betrotheds.

And as for the other nonsense he'd been talking—about how maybe the betrothal would not be a pretence—well, that was just ridiculous. He was the ruler of his country. He might have joked about a suitable marriage for the good of his camels, but surely, in all seriousness, there would be certain expectations of him in regard to marriage—either political or familial—and she doubted she'd be considered suitable by any of his advisors or power-brokers.

She buried her face in her hands. 'Oh, Pop, what have you got me into?' she whispered, but Pop was a million miles away and hopefully in hospital so he was no help. She'd just have to sort this out on her own.

Why in the name of fortune was he doing this? The question lurked in the back of Ghazi's brain as he talked with supplicants who had been given lunch while waiting for his final decisions on their claims. His officials looked into all the claims then gave him their opinions so he could make a judgment. He discussed land rights, and the sale of camels, and fixed a bride price for the father of a young woman keen to marry out of her family—marry a foreigner, in fact.

Ironic, that! Should he be offering a bride price to Marni's grandfather?

Marni!

Her name sang its way into his conscious mind and he needed Mazur's discreet cough to bring him back to the subject at hand—an altercation over the placement of two stalls in the souk.

'Your families have worked stalls side by side for generations,' he told the two men sitting cross-legged in front of him. 'Why the trouble now?'

'It's his daughter,' one said.

In chorus with, 'It's his son,' from the second man.

'They like each other?' Ghazi guessed.

'Too much,' the father of the daughter spat. 'But she is already betrothed to a distant cousin— from when she was four—but young people these days!'

The situation was far too close to this morning's astonishing revelations, and he was feeling more and more uncomfortable as the two men explained all the reasons why their children should not marry, and therefore why their stalls should be moved so the young people were not in constant contact.

'A betrothal at such a young age need not stand,' Ghazi said cautiously, ignoring the fact that he was pushing for just such a betrothal to stand in his own situation. 'Times have changed, my friends, and if these two love each other, instead of fighting, can you not put your heads together and work out a way for them to marry and be happy? After all, you could then combine your stalls and have twice the space and twice the customers, surely. I could possibly arrange extra space for the expanded stall, by way of a marriage gift for the couple.'

Behind him, he heard Mazur's sharp intake of breath, and knew he'd overstepped some invisible barrier, but if the two young people were genuinely in love...

He heard the phrase—genuinely in love—echo in his head and wondered if he'd lost his mind.

'I want to see both of them,' he said, 'to hear from them how they feel. Make sure they are at the next citizens' meeting.'

Thus dismissed, the two men departed, united now, he had no doubt, in horror over what he had suggested.

'Genuinely in love!' Mazur mocked. 'What on earth has got into you, Ghazi? Since when was love a factor in the settlement of disputes? Or in marriage, for that matter?'

Ghazi turned to the man who was not only his first advisor but also his best friend, aware he had to be careful.

'We must move with the times, Mazur,' he said. 'You know full well that the system of arranged marriages is not infallible—many such marriages fail and many of our people seek and are granted divorces. Maybe marrying for love will be more successful—and don't start quoting me figures from the West where people do it all the time. I know about their divorce rates. But young people have always longed for love, so surely if they find it, can we deny it to them? Can we break up two families by standing in the way of these young people?'

He was obviously losing his mind, Ghazi decided as Mazur gave a disbelieving snort and walked away.

Surely it couldn't have been the couple of kisses he'd shared with Marni that had him turning an age-old tradition on its head.

Marrying for love?

No wonder Mazur was snorting.

Marni packed her things then sat on the bed in the small bedroom and tried to work out exactly what she was doing.

And why.

If you're finding it hard to make a decision, write a list, Pop had always said. That was how she'd decided which university to attend, which course to take, even, one slightly embarrassing time, which of two young men would take her to the hospital ball.

So, mentally, she made her list.

For going along with Gaz—Ghazi—on this betrothal thing was that she would be doing him a favour, and it was never a bad thing to have a favour owed.

Besides, Nelson had said he'd been a nice little boy who'd been very kind to her at a time when she'd been desperately alone and confused, so maybe *she* owed *him* one.

Then there was Pop, who'd be delighted, and by the time the betrothal ended, however they were to manage that, he'd be over the operation so could handle the news without too much of a problem.

And…

She couldn't think of an and!

Well, she could, but she'd already decided he probably wouldn't seduce her while they were betrothed.

Against—well, that was easy. The disruption in her life for a start, the hassle of whatever the betrothal would entail in the way of public appearances, the interruption to her work, having to get new clothes—

She smiled to herself and wondered if that should go on the 'for' list…

Then there was Gaz.

Was he a for or against?

A bit of both really, because as Gaz she liked him and more than liked his kisses, but as Ghazi, wasn't there something wrong with kissing him if their betrothal was only pretend?

Fayyad would be wondering what had become of her, but still she sat, looking down at her watch as she tried to work out what time it would be at home.

If she phoned Nelson, she could ask him what he thought, ask him what she should do, as she'd always asked him what to do, relying on his common sense and good judgement.

But Nelson had enough on his plate right now, looking after Pop, so she was on her own.

She stood up, grabbed her suitcase and made her way down to the foyer and out to the door, where Fayyad waited patiently in the car, climbing out when he saw her to open the back door for her.

'I need to stop at the hospital to see a patient,' she told him, feeling guilty because with all the 'will I, won't I' that had gone on in her head about attending the citizens' meeting she hadn't seen Safi for two days. 'I'll be half an hour, maybe a little more. Do you have to wait in the car, or can you go into the canteen and have a cool drink or a coffee?'

Fayyad smiled at her then lifted a Thermos and a book to show her.

'I am never bored while waiting,' he said, 'but thank you for your consideration.'

His English was so good she wanted to ask where he'd learned it but remembered that personal conversations seemed not actually forbidden but perhaps impolite. She must ask Gaz.

Ask Gaz?

Just because he'd kissed her it didn't mean…

Didn't mean what?

And surely the kisses hadn't made her feel more at ease with him than she did with Jawa, for instance?

Totally muddled, she watched as Fayyad pulled up in front of the hospital.

'I will be watching for you,' he said, as he opened the door for her, making her feel a total fool. She thanked him and hurried inside, hoping none of the nurses she knew had seen her stately arrival. But the staff entrance was around the back so she should be safe.

These niggling worries hung around her like a cloud of summer midges as she walked towards Safi's room, but vanished as soon as she entered. She'd vaguely been aware of intense activity in one of the rooms she'd passed, and a lot of scurrying further down the passageway, but surely whatever was going on, someone would have checked on Safi recently.

His face was pale but red spots of fever burned in his cheeks and his thin fingers plucked at the dressing on his lip while his body turned and twisted on the bed.

'Safi!' she said, coming to take the hand that worried at his dressing, feeling the heat of it.

She found the bell and pressed it, then grabbed a towel and ran water over it in the little attached bathroom, wringing it out then bringing it back to sponge his face and chest, his arms and legs, desperate to cool him down before the spike in his temperature could cause a seizure.

No one had answered the bell.

She pressed it again, talking soothingly to the little boy, careful not to touch the dressing as his wound was obviously causing him discomfort, or more likely, pain.

He was staring up at her, wide-eyed, panic and pain in equal measure in his face.

'It will be all right,' she said, and although

she knew he wouldn't understand her words she hoped her voice would soothe him. Her voice and the cool, wet towel...

Wrapping the towel around his head like a turban so it pressed on his temples and the back of his neck and could cool surface blood vessels in both places, she grabbed his chart. Thankfully all charts were written in English because of the imported staff, and although she couldn't read exactly what he'd been given at the last check, she could tell that it had been at ten in the morning.

Had no one seen the child since then, apart from ward cleaners and the maid who'd carried in the meal that was uneaten on his table?

Giving up on the bell, she carried the chart out into the corridor, heading for the nurses' station, needing urgent attention for Safi and ready to demand answers.

The place was deserted, although she could tell there was still a major commotion in one of the rooms she'd passed earlier and a fair level of noise coming from a room further up the corridor.

There had to be a nurse in one of those rooms.

Three nurses and two doctors, in fact, and a crash cart pushed to one side.

'She just went flat,' the nurse Marni hauled into the corridor explained, 'about two hours ago. The doctors thought we'd lost her but she's coming round now.'

Marni accepted it had been an emergency but that only accounted for three of the nursing staff.

Not that she had time to complain! She hurried the nurse towards Safi's room.

'I came to visit, and there he was, burning with fever.'

'Oh, not Safi!' the nurse wailed. 'I'll have to page Gaz—he insists on knowing any change in Safi's condition—and get a ward doctor in as well. Can you go back and sit with Safi for a few minutes?'

She looked about her and frowned as if she'd just become aware of the emptiness of the corridor and nurses' station.

'I've no idea where the others are,' she added, peering vaguely around.

'I don't care where they are,' Marni snapped. 'I just need someone to see Safi and see him now.'

She might have raised her voice just slightly, but she was pretty sure she'd kept it below a shout, which was what she'd really wanted to do.

Hurrying back to Safi's room, she wet the now warm towel and bathed him again, pressing the cold cloth on his wrists and in his elbow joints, below his knees and against his neck and head, talking all the time, wishing she knew his language, wishing she would somehow conjure up his mother for him, for his little body was now slack, his eyes closed—the fight gone out of him.

The nurse came in and Marni stepped back while the woman checked his pulse, temperature and blood pressure, then a young doctor appeared, looked at the figures and fiddled with the drip, checking the catheter in the back of Sufi's thin hand, making sure the tape was in place.

'I've been off duty for a few days but I know that since the wound in his hip where they took the bone from has healed quite well, he's been walking around the hospital, even going outside at times. He must have picked up an infection,' the nurse suggested as the doctor drew blood for testing.

An infection that could cause such a rapid response?

Marni wondered about it but said nothing—in this room she was a visitor.

And she was still angry that the rise in his temperature hadn't been picked up earlier, before he'd become so distressed.

Gaz's arrival provided answers. He must have been on the phone during his journey from the palace to the hospital, telling her, as he examined Safi, that apart from the child who'd needed resuscitation, an accident to a school bus had brought a rush of, thankfully, minor injuries to the hospital, diverting staff to the ER, then to top it off the mother of another patient in the post-op ward had gone into labour and actually given birth in her daughter's hospital room.

'Still no excuse,' Marni thought she heard him mutter, but the barely heard words were followed by a rush of orders, arranging for Safi to go straight to Theatre.

'But with his fever—with the infection still so active?' Marni protested.

Gaz shrugged.

'Unfortunately yes. His temperature rose the day before yesterday and we've had him on vancomycin, which is usually the most effective drug for multi-resistant bacteria, but it obviously isn't working. I need to remove the grafted bone before the infection spreads into good bone.'

He paused for a moment, then said, 'There are still staff problems. Will you scrub?'

'Of course!'

An orderly appeared to wheel Safi to Theatre and Marni backed out of his room so he could be moved, waiting until he was wheeled out then falling in behind the little procession.

Gaz was walking beside the gurney and turned to glance back at the woman who'd erupted into his life, spinning it in a direction he'd never expected it to take—well, not right now.

She'd come from what must have been a fairly momentous day, given the job he was thrusting her into, to see a child she barely knew, and now was quite happy to spend however many hours it would take in Theatre for Gaz to remove the bone graft because there was no way the infection could be anywhere else.

She'd stripped off the abaya and was wearing jeans and a loose shirt, and just the sight of her stirred thoughts he shouldn't be having right now.

'I suppose the infection can't be anywhere but in the graft?'

Marni had caught up and was walking beside him, but apparently her mind was still firmly fixed on Safi. Gaz swung his mind back that way, determined to concentrate no matter how distracting he found his colleague.

'The site's red and swollen and obviously painful. The nurse who changed his dressing this morning should have noticed and alerted someone.'

'I wondered,' Marni said, 'but I didn't like to touch it.'

'You did enough, cooling him down and alerting the staff. Without you—'

He stopped, so angry, so upset for the little boy he needed his own language—and bad words from it—to release his rage.

But not at Marni!

'Thank you for being there—for caring enough to call in to see him,' he said, and lifted his hand to touch her on the shoulder. 'From me and from Safi!'

She didn't move away from his touch but turned towards him, the slight frown he'd seen before creasing the smooth creamy skin of her brow—and even a frown caused inappropriate reactions.

'But he's been on antibiotics since the operation—I saw that on his chart—and you've started stronger antibiotics—would they not work in time?'

Gaz shrugged.

'I daren't take the risk. Yes, there's risk involved operating when he's harbouring something bad, but...'

He sighed, before adding, 'I thought because our hospital is so new we'd avoid things like this for a few more years. The problem is that so many of the bad ones target bone, and the grafted bone is likely to be badly compromised.'

The crease in his companion's forehead deepened.

'So you'll take the graft out, then how long before you could do another one? You'd have to clear the infection first, and where could you harvest the bone? His other hip?'

Her mind was obviously more focussed than his had been—no inappropriate reactions for Marni!

'I'll take it out, that's enough for Safi today. Later, when we know he's clear of infection, yes, I'll have to harvest some new bone and, yes, probably from his other hip. Poor lad. He's been through so much and bears it all so bravely. I'd have done anything to have saved him from this.'

They'd stopped in the corridor outside the theatre changing rooms; the orderly and nurse pushing Sufi's gurney moved on and through the theatre's swing doors.

'Will he be able to go home to his family before the next op?'

Gaz studied her for a moment, so aware of her as a woman it was hard to concentrate on the question she was asking.

'And why do you wish to know?'

A faint colour rose in her cheeks.

'Well, if you must know, although I genuinely care about Safi and want what's best for him, I'm so darned confused about all that's happened today, and then walking along beside you as if *nothing* had happened, well, it seemed best just to keep talking about practical things rather than have a fit of hysterics in the hospital corridor.'

Her cheeks grew pinker and her eyes dropped to study the floor between their feet, and he felt an overwhelming urge to give her a hug—a big hug, a warm hug, a non-sexy hug, although how long the non-sexy part would last was a moot point.

'Me too,' he said, ignoring the urge. He touched her lightly on the elbow and waved her through the door into the changing rooms.

He'd obviously made good use of his time during his trip from the palace to the hospital, for an anaesthetist Marni had worked with before was already attending to Sufi, talking quietly to him as he set his drip on a stand and prepared to give him a pre-op sedative.

Jawa was also there and greeted Marni warmly, although she did raise her eyebrows.

'But you're off duty,' she murmured.

'And doing me a favour.'

It was Gaz who answered for her, coming into the theatre behind her.

'It is Marni who found Safi so ill,' Gaz added, causing Jawa to look from him to Marni, so many questions in her beautiful dark eyes Marni knew she'd have some explaining to do later.

Personal explaining, for all it might go against the local custom!

Three hours later, Safi was wheeled away to Recovery, the open wound where the graft having been cleaned out and left with a drain in it to leach out any more of the poison. Marni felt tears prick at her eyelids and knew it was tiredness—well, tiredness and the stress of the totally bizarre day, *and* her heartache for little Safi, who had already suffered so much, and underlying it all her worry over Pop...

Gaz caught her arm as she was about to follow Jawa out of Theatre. He'd pulled his mask down so it hung loosely below his chin, and the fine line of beard was a little ragged. His eyes, however, still held her gaze, drawing her into the darkness...

'You are exhausted,' he said gently. 'I would

suggest you go back to your flat here at the hospital but Fayyad tells me all your things are in the car. Let me drive you to Tasnim's. She is expecting you and will have waited up for you.'

Marni dragged her attention back from his eyes and nodded, too tired to argue, and anyway he was right, all her belongings were in the car. She slipped into the changing room, and again saw the questions in Jawa's eyes.

'Tomorrow,' she said to her friend. 'I'll return your abaya and explain tomorrow. I'll meet you at the canteen at ten.'

But could she explain?

Explain it all?

And how would a local woman feel about her ruler's betrothal to a foreigner?

Not to mention if she said it was a pretence.

So many questions to which she had no answers…

The ruler in question was waiting for her in the corridor.

'Is it going to cause you problems with your people, this betrothal?' she asked as soon as she was close to him. 'I know it seemed like a good idea at the time to get your sisters off your back, but what about the local population? Might they not be offended in some way? Feel I've cheated you, or you them?'

Gaz—he was definitely Gaz at the hospital—stared at her for a moment then shook his head.

'Do you worry over everybody?' he asked, the smile in his eyes, and somehow in his voice as well, making her stomach curl.

'Of course not, but Jawa must be wondering what's going on and I wouldn't like—well, she's been so kind to me, I really have to try to explain to her before you do this breaking me to the public gradually business, and then I thought—'

He brushed his knuckles across her cheek and her mind went blank.

'That I might be lynched, or deposed, for getting betrothed to a foreigner?'

Marni managed to nod, but with Gaz so close and the sensation of that touch lingering on her cheek, she found it impossible to speak.

Or think.

And only just possible to breathe.

'Stop fretting,' he told her, 'and that's an order!'

He then put his hand gently on the small of her back—again—and propelled her down the corridor, into the car and out again only minutes later, in front of the low open patio of a house the size of a hotel.

Tasnim was a short, glowing, heavily pregnant woman wearing designer jeans—who knew designers made pregnancy jeans?—and a tight purple top stretched across her swollen abdomen.

She greeted Marni with a warm hug and made no secret of her delight.

'This will be such fun!' she said. 'I was bored out of my brain. I did keep working but got so fat I couldn't sit behind the desk any more and Yusef—Ghazi's told you he's my husband, hasn't he?—said to stop, then the wretched man took off to Europe for some round of international monetary fund talks and just left me stranded here.'

Marni could only stare at the beautiful, bubbly, excited woman.

'She *can* talk,' Gaz said, giving his sister a kiss on the cheek and asking where Fayyad should put Marni's luggage.

'Oh, Ahmed will take it.'

Tasnim waved her hand towards a white-clad figure and the luggage disappeared.

'But are you sure this is okay?' Marni finally managed to ask. 'Me being here, I mean?'

'Of course,' Tasnim told her, giving her another awkward hug. 'Not only will I have the fun of getting clothes for you—and spending lots and lots of Ghazi's money—but every one of my sisters will be green with jealousy that you're here and not with them.'

She clapped her hands.

'Oh, it will be delicious!'

'But I wouldn't want your sisters—' Marni began.

'Don't worry,' Gaz told her, resting his hand on her shoulder. 'They play these games of one-up-manship all the time, my sisters, but they still all love each other. Just wait, they'll be vying with each other to give you the best gifts, take you to the best silk shops, the best seamstresses.'

Marni closed her eyes as she realised this whole betrothal thing had spun right out of control and taken on a life of its own. She turned to Gaz so his hand fell off her shoulder, which did make it slightly easier to think.

'I can't take gifts,' she said, which was as close as she could get to protesting in front of Tasnim. 'It wouldn't be right!'

'Of course it's right,' Tasnim argued. 'You're his betrothed.'

But it's pretend! Marni wanted to yell, and as she couldn't, she made do with a glare at the man who'd got her into this situation.

Well, it had been partly her fault...

Perhaps mostly her fault...

'She's exhausted,' she heard Gaz say. 'What she needs is food, a bath and bed, and no teasing her for explanations or gossip or any chat at all!'

'Yes, Master,' Tasnim teased, 'but don't think I'm going to turn round while you kiss her good-bye. We've all been waiting far too long for you to fall for someone.'

He hasn't fallen for me, it's all pretence, Marni wanted to say, but didn't because even thinking about it made her feel a little sad and, anyway, Gaz was obviously giving his sister a piece of his mind, so stern did his words sound. Then, with one last touch on Marni's shoulder, he stalked away.

'Come,' Tasnim said. 'I won't tease you.'

She took Marni's hand and led her through a bewildering maze of corridors, across carpets with glowing jewel colours, through arches with decorative plaster picked out in gold and set with precious stones. The rooms she'd seen in the palace had been plain, though there, too, the carpets had been beautiful, but this was like some fantasy out of an old-fashioned book and, tired as she was, it took on a dream-like quality.

'Here!' Tasnim finally said, going ahead of Marni into a room the size of her entire hospital flat. A huge four-poster bed, hung with dark blue silk curtains, dominated one end of the room while the inner walls were lined with a paler blue silk, padded somehow and indented with buttons of the same colour.

'The bathroom is through that door and a dressing room through the one next to it. You'll find plenty of clothes in the dressing room because we like our guests to feel comfortable and sometimes they may not have brought clothing that will fit special occasions.'

She flung open a door into what looked like a very expensive boutique. A long rack down one side held clothes ranging from ballgowns to tailored shirts and skirts, while further down were jeans and slacks and even, she rather thought, some long shorts.

The other side of the room had shelves of shoe-boxes and drawers containing exotic-looking underwear, still in its original packaging, and beyond the drawers long, filmy nightdresses.

For the harem—no, seraglio—belly dancers? was Marni's immediate thought. Wasn't this proof they still existed?

'Not that you need any fancy clothes here,' Tasnim was saying. 'Wear whatever you like. Now I'm pregnant, I do cover up with an abaya if I go into the city, but I always worked in Western clothes.'

Marni wanted to ask what work she did, to find out more about this lively, fascinating young woman, but tiredness had fallen on her like a great weight.

'Have a bath and go to bed, Tasnim ordered. 'I'll have a light meal sent up to you—just eat what you want. Tomorrow we'll talk.

'Thank you,' Marni said. 'I *am* tired.'

CHAPTER SIX

SHE'D ENTERED A world of fantasy, Marni realised when she woke in the luxuriously soft four-poster bed to find a young woman sitting cross-legged by the door, obviously waiting for the visitor to open her eyes.

'Good morning, I hope you slept well,' the young woman said, rising to her feet with elegant smoothness. 'I am Shara and I am to look after you. I shall bring you whatever you wish— some tea or coffee to begin with perhaps, then you must tell me what you wish for breakfast. Ms Tasnim sleeps late and has her breakfast in bed.'

'A cup of tea would be wonderful,' Marni told her. 'English tea if you have it. I can drink mint tea later in the day but need the tea I'm used to to wake me up.'

The girl smiled and disappeared, her bare feet making no sound on the marble floor, although

Marni fancied she could hear the swish of the soft material of the girl's long trousers and the long tunic she wore over them.

Marni had a quick shower and, aware of her appointment with Jawa at the hospital, dressed in one of the pairs of loose trousers she'd brought from home, adding a tunic in her favourite deep blue-green colour.

'You dress like us?' Shara commented when she returned with the tea.

'I decided before I left home that if I was going out in public it would be polite to follow the local customs,' Marni told her. 'In my flat, and possibly while I'm staying here, inside the house, I might pull on my jeans.'

'I am the opposite, I wear jeans outside,' Shara said. 'This is just a uniform for work.'

Marni sipped at her tea, wanting to know more—about Shara, about Ablezia, about—

'You speak such good English,' she said. 'Did you learn it at school?'

'At school and at college too, and I listen to recordings at home as well. I am training to work in hotels, you see. We are building many hotels now in our country and they will all need staff. One day, I would like to manage one, but first I must learn the basics of housekeeping, then I must learn how to run a kitchen, not to cook but to understand what goes on, then—oh, there is so much to learn.'

She flashed a bright smile at Marni, who smiled back as she said, 'You'll go far, I'm sure.'

'Not if I don't get a breakfast order from you,' Shara said, still smiling. 'The chef will have my head. What would you like?'

What would she like?

'What do you have for breakfast?' she asked.

'You would like to try a local breakfast?' Shara asked, obviously delighted.

'As long as it doesn't take too long to prepare. I have to be at the hospital at ten.'

Shara disappeared, returning with a round brass tray on which nestled six small bowls. In the middle of the tray round flatbread was folded into cones, the whole thing like some wonderful display made for a picture in a food magazine.

'Here,' Shara said, as she set it on the small table by an arched window. She pulled a plate out from under the bread and a napkin from beneath that again, and waited for Marni to sit. She then pointed to each dish in turn.

'This is labneh, our cheese, a bit tangy but soft, and dahl, you know dahl from lentils, and these are eggs mixed up and cooked with spices, some olives, some hummus, and here is honey, and jam, apricot, I think, and halwa—you know the sweet halwa?'

'It looks fantastic but I can't possibly eat it all,' Marni protested, and Shara laughed.

'You just eat a little of whatever you want. You use the bread to scoop it up or there is cutlery on the plate if you prefer to use that. Now, we would drink tea but tea you have had, so perhaps coffee?'

Marni agreed that she'd like coffee and as Shara disappeared once more, Marni began to eat, scooping bits of one dish, then another, trying them alone, then together, settling on the spicy eggs and labneh as her main choices and eating far more than she normally would for breakfast.

Coffee and dates finished the meal, and as she was thanking Shara, Tasnim burst into the room.

'I've come to make plans,' she announced, but before she could continue Marni explained she was meeting Jawa—and soon.

'Oh!' Tasnim was deflated but not for long. 'That is good. I send you with a driver in the car to the hospital and when you are finished with your friend he will bring you to the Plaza Hotel. The shops there are discreet and we can enjoy shopping without a crowd.'

'The Plaza?' Marni echoed faintly, thinking of the enormous, palace-like hotel she'd seen but had never visited.

'Definitely the Plaza, it is the only place,' Tasnim insisted, before whirling out of the room to make arrangements for a driver.

'You will like the Plaza,' Shara said, her voice so full of awe Marni felt even more uncertain.

'Have you been there?' she asked the girl.

'Oh, no, but I hear it is very beautiful and the boutiques there—well, they are for the very rich.'

Which you obviously are not. Marni felt she could hear Shara's thoughts. She'd know that from unpacking her suitcase.

Marni ignored the questions she'd heard in

Shara's voice. She grabbed a scarf to wrap around her hair, found her handbag, then asked Shara to take her to wherever the driver would be waiting with the car.

'I daren't walk out of the room for fear of getting lost,' she told the girl, who smiled but was still treating her with more reserve than she had originally.

Treating her like someone who shopped at the Plaza!

Hell's teeth, Marni thought. Does money really change things so much?

She was early when she arrived at the hospital, so her feet took her automatically to Safi's room. The little boy was sleeping, but she'd barely registered that when her body told her who else was visiting him, although the second person had been in the bathroom, washing his hands, as she'd come in.

He was in full prince gear, so—pathetically— her breath caught in her lungs and her heart stopped beating.

'You look beautiful,' Gaz—no, he was definitely Ghazi—said, crossing the room towards

her and taking her hands. 'You slept well? Tasnim is looking after you?'

He raised her hands to his lips and kissed each
knuckle in turn, making it impossible for her to
answer him.

Soft footsteps in the corridor made him release
her hands and step back, but the look in his eyes
was enough to bring all the embers of desire back
to ferocious life.

Why *wasn't* he just Gaz?

'How is Safi?' Marni asked, in an attempt to
dampen the heat.

'He is well, his temperature is down and his
sleep is peaceful,' he replied, then he lifted one
of her hands, dropped a kiss on the palm and left
the room, muttering to himself.

It had to be the stupidest idea he'd ever had, he
decided as he marched away from Safi's room.
Here was a woman he desired more than he'd
ever desired a woman before and he'd put her off
limits by becoming betrothed to her.

And all to avoid the women his sisters were
throwing at him!

But could he have accepted any of them, feeling as he did about Marni?

And how *did* he feel about Marni?

He desired her but was that it? Would an affair have satisfied that desire? Could they have shared some mutual pleasure and enjoyment then parted?

He wasn't too sure about that.

There was something about the woman. She was different, and not only in race but in…

Personality?

Guts?

It had taken guts to approach him yesterday, not knowing who he was or what might occur, but she'd done it for her grandfather…

He needed to know her better. He'd go back to Safi's room now.

'Sir!'

One of the junior doctors had caught up with him and tapped him lightly on the shoulder. Had he called to him more than once?

'Your driver, sir, he has a message for you.'

Back to reality! Gaz strode towards the front entrance, aware his driver would only have sent for him if he was already late for the next thing on his interminable schedule.

Marni held the kiss in her hand as she made her way to the canteen. She felt slightly foolish. The kiss meant nothing so why hold onto it?

Did she want it to mean something?

Want it to mean love?

She shook her head at her thoughts and smiled sadly. Six times so far her mother had married for 'love' so, not unnaturally, Marni had a slightly skewed view of it.

The advent of lust into her life had really confused things, she decided as she dawdled down the corridor. Caught up in its snare, couldn't one mistake it for love?

Want it to be love?

Was that what had happened with her mother?

Again and again and…

She sighed, and put the problem out of her mind. Right now she had to get her head straight and work out exactly what she was going to say to Jawa.

Jawa!

Jawa meant passion or love—Marni had looked it up when she'd learned that most names had meanings. Ghazi—of course she'd looked it up as well—meant conqueror.

Hmmm!

Jawa was waiting in the canteen, two cups of coffee and a plate of sweet pastries on the table in front of her. Marni slipped into a chair opposite so she could look into her friend's face as she spoke.

The politeness of morning greetings and thanks for the coffee held off the revelations for a few minutes but finally she had to tackle the subject she'd come to discuss.

'You know I've mentioned Pop, my grandfather,' she began, then stalled.

'Your grandfather?' Jawa prompted.

'It's complicated, but I didn't know when I met him in Theatre that Gaz was Ghazi, your prince. The thing is, Pop had known him and his father when he was a boy—when Ghazi was a boy— and Pop wanted me to say hello to him while I was here, which was why I borrowed your abaya and went to the palace yesterday, and now we're kind of engaged to help him out with his sisters who keep finding women for him to marry.'

Jawa's eyes had grown rounder and rounder as Marni's disjointed explanation had stumbled from her lips.

'You're engaged to Prince Ghazi?' Jawa whispered, her voice ripe with disbelief.

'Only pretend—for his sisters,' Marni said desperately, but she rather thought that message wasn't getting through. 'And we're keeping it quiet but I've moved in to live with his pregnant sister, for security he says.'

It wasn't making much sense to Marni so she had no idea what Jawa might be making of it.

'The thing is, I don't know what his people—people like you—will think about it, because he should probably be marrying with better breeding stock for his camels.'

Drained now of words, Marni stared hopefully at Jawa, who seemed to have gone into some kind of fugue, although she did manage a faint echo.

'Camels?'

'So what do you think?' Marni eventually demanded, the silence adding to the tension already built up inside her.

'About the camels?' Jawa said faintly.

'No, not the camels, although apparently his camels are very important to him, but about me being engaged to him—betrothed?'

Jawa shook her head.

'I don't know what to think but if it's been arranged—your grandfather and his father—then that's how things should be. I know more of our people are marrying for love these days but arranged marriages have worked for centuries.'

'I'm not *marrying* him,' Marni told her. 'It's a pretend betrothal—because of his sisters—just while he sorts out his job—and then...'

'And then?' Jawa probed.

Marni shrugged.

'I have no idea,' she said. 'It's really all just too stupid for words, but I felt I should tell you because you've been so good to me. I'd like to keep working but we don't seem to have talked too much about that. Tasnim—that's his sister—seems to think clothes are more important.'

'Oh, clothes will be very important,' Jawa said, then she smiled and took Marni's hand.

'I only know him when he's Gaz, of course, as a colleague. He is much respected and admired. From the time he started work here, he has never made anything of his links with the ruling family and no one ever treated him any differently because of who he is. I don't think he expected to take over from his uncle, but he will do his duty well.'

Of course he will, Marni thought, feeling slightly let down, although she wasn't sure what she'd expected of this conversation.

Congratulations?

Certainly not!

Reassurance?

Of course!

'It's the pretence that bothers me,' she said. 'Will people—the local people—be upset when it ends?'

Jawa thought for a moment then turned Marni's hand in hers.

'I do not think so. They will accept his decision, whatever it is. Those who thought it was a bad idea to marry a foreigner will say at last he's come to his senses, and those who liked the idea will think, ah, that's the trouble with love because they will have been sure it was a love match.'

A love match?

For some reason, far from reassuring her, the words sent a wave of melancholy washing over Marni and she took back her hand—it wasn't the one with the kiss in it—and sighed.

Love, of course, was the other reason she had the virginity problem—her mother's version of love…

The Plaza Hotel was surely bigger than the palace!

That was Marni's first thought on seeing it as they drove up a long drive to an immense building spread across the top of a slight rise.

And far more opulent, she realised as she entered the enormous lobby so gilded and arched and carpeted it looked more like a posh showroom of some kind than a hotel.

Tasnim was waiting, perched on a chair beside a lounge setting.

'Would you believe they don't have ordinary chairs like this in the lobby?' she demanded, when she'd greeted Marni with a kiss on the cheek. 'I had to ask someone to find one for me. There's no way I could have stood up from one of those low, soft sofas without making a total fool of myself.'

Marni smiled, doubting the formidable Tasnim could ever make a fool of herself anywhere.

'Come,' Tasnim continued. 'We'll be given refreshments in the boutique. I phoned ahead and asked for my favourite one to be closed for us. The women from the other boutiques will come there with whatever else we need.'

A shop closed so she could shop? Once again Marni found herself in fantasy land.

'I've made a list,' Tasnim told her. 'I thought half a dozen everyday things for a start. Just things like you're wearing today so your way of dressing doesn't offend anyone. Then half a dozen formal outfits—two kinds—Western for entertaining diplomats and other foreigners, and Eastern for entertaining locals. And some casual clothes for at home and for when Ghazi visits.'

'I have my own clothes for at home,' Marni protested as they entered the boutique, a woman bowing them through the door.

'Nonsense! You can't be wearing the same thing every time you see Ghazi, now, can you?'

Couldn't she?

Marni felt a little lump of sadness lodged beneath her breast.

Because she knew Ghazi didn't really care *what* she was wearing?

Probably!

Although he *had* said she looked beautiful this morning…

The lump remained.

Tasnim was talking to the saleswoman, the words rattling around the beautifully set-up salon.

Marni was checked out, looked up and down, ordered to turn around, then told to sit on a low love seat and offered tea.

She shook her head and looked about her. There was only one gown on display—a Western evening gown made of some silvery material, and sewn with beads and crystals so it shimmered under a discreetly placed light.

It appeared perfectly simple in style and cut and yet was breathtakingly beautiful.

'Local things first,' Tasnim declared, returning with the saleswoman and a young woman who was pushing a trolley hung with clothes, spectacular clothes in rich greens and blues, long loose trousers, patterned and beaded tunics that would go over them and at the end of the rack a selection of black abayas.

An hour later, Marni was the rather hesitant possessor of four new pairs of trousers and five new tunics. She'd put her foot down over Tasnim's suggestion she'd need half a dozen, listened in disbelief as Tasnim and the saleswoman claimed to have hundreds of such outfits, and had been talked into the fifth tunic because it was so beautiful.

It was the simplest of them all, not bright but a pale blue-grey with a pearl-coloured thread woven through it and the patterning around the bottom in the pointy-topped shape of the local arches, picked out in darker blue.

As for the abayas! Far from the plain cotton garment she'd borrowed from Jawa, these were woven from the finest silk, with delicate ebony bead embroidery around the hem, sleeves and neckline. Beautiful garments to cover other beautiful garments.

The fantasy deepened!

'If you choose a couple with hoods, it will save you tying a tight scarf over your hair when you go out,' Tasnim advised. 'Abayas used not to have hoods as we wore a hijab—a specially tied scarf—over our heads. But with the hoods, any of your scarves would go under the hood.'

The saleswoman hung the abaya Marni had tried for size back on the rack—on the buying side, not the reject side—and studied Marni yet again.

'Surely that's enough for one day,' she begged Tasnim, but her new friend wouldn't be distracted.

'We haven't done the scarves,' she scolded. 'If you're insisting on only having four outfits, at least you can vary them with scarves.'

Long scarves, as fine as gossamer, were produced, most in tantalising colours, all embroidered in different ways.

She was wearing the tunic she'd been unable to resist, and the woman found a scarf in the darker blue of the embroidery and draped it around Marni's head and shoulders.

'Perfect. It makes your skin gleam like alabaster and turns your eyes as blue as cornflowers,' Tasnim said, clapping her hands in delight. 'But you will need more. Darker ones are good for evening, and if you have a darker one over your hair, you can still tie it hijab style and need not pull the hood of the abaya over your head.'

Marni assumed Tasnim was talking sense but she was lost. She found herself drifting, doing whatever Tasnim or the saleslady told her, lost in the mad dream that had become her life.

The evening gowns were unbelievable—like things she'd seen actresses wearing on the red carpet when the Oscars were televised. And the names of the designers—names she'd heard with awe and had never in her wildest dreams imagined wearing clothes they'd designed.

But she was also tiring fast and after trying on and removing the sixth evening gown she found the energy to protest.

'Tasnim, we've settled on three, that's enough,' she said, although her eyes strayed to the silver creation on the shop model.

Tasnim saw her look that way then she said, 'Just one more,' and spoke to the saleswoman, who immediately began disrobing the manne-quin.

'It's made for you with your fair skin and hair,' Tasnim insisted, and when Marni put it on she knew she had to have it. She'd never considered herself beautiful, but in this dress?

She remembered Gaz saying after dinner at the hospital that she was like a silver wraith—well, in this dress she almost was.

So why was that lump back in her chest and her heart hurting, just a little bit?

'Sandals next,' Tasnim decreed, and another saleswoman appeared pushing a trolley laden with shoeboxes. Marni gave up. She pushed her feet in and out of sandals, stood in them, walked around, and finally settled on a few pairs, al-though it seemed Tasnim was making her own decisions as at least ten boxes were piled together while the rest were wheeled away.

But when make-up and perfume were suggested, Marni stood her ground.

'I can handle that myself,' she said firmly. 'I have my own make-up and have always used the same perfume, a particular scent my grandfather first bought me when I was eighteen. I'm not changing that!'

Tasnim argued she needed more than one so she could choose according to the time of day and the occasion and the outfit, but Marni was adamant—she'd wear her own, any time, any day, anywhere!

Exhausted by the decision-making, all she wanted to do was go home—well, back to Tasnim's place, and lie on the bed, and try to make sense of all that had happened to her.

Although wasn't that bed part of the fantasy?

But Tasnim was ruthless.

'Of course we can't go home,' she said. 'We need to go over to the palace and get you some jewellery. Ghazi won't want people thinking he's too mean to give you jewellery and until he's got time to buy you some, there's a ton of stuff over there. Some of it's a bit old-fashioned, which is why we sisters all insisted our husbands bought us more—but we all got plenty of the family stuff in our bridal chests.'

Marni stopped outside the boutique to study the woman who'd taken over her life.

'Aren't pregnant women supposed to get tired and to need a lot of rest?' she demanded.

'Oh, phooey,' Tasnim replied. 'You sound like my mother. I'll rest later!'

So, to the palace they went, Marni regretting she hadn't stayed in one of her new outfits in case they ran into Ghazi, but that was stupid, wasn't it?

Once at the palace, Tasnim summoned Mazur and must have explained what they wanted for he led them through more tortuous passages, finally unlocking what looked like, but couldn't possibly have been, a solid gold door. Pulling a huge, old-fashioned key from beneath his kandora, he unlocked the door, pressed numbers on a very modern-looking security system pad, then turned on a light to reveal an Aladdin's cave of riches.

'Oh!'

Marni breathed the word, unable to believe

that a picture from a childhood book could be springing to life in front of her. Yes, there were neat chests with little drawers in them, and glass cabinets with displays of stunning jewellery, but there were also open chests and large jars from which spilled what looked like all the treasures of the world.

'The children like to play with the chests and jars,' Mazur explained in a very disapproving voice. He was retrieving a long string of pearls from the floor as he spoke, and examining them for damage.

'But I couldn't possibly wear any of this kind of jewellery,' Marni protested. 'I'd look ridiculous!'

'So start simple,' the indomitable Tasnim told her. 'Take those pearls, for instance. They will go beautifully with that tunic you really like. Mazur, a bracelet or bangle to go with them and a ring, of course.'

Mazur poked through drawers, finally emerging with a bracelet that had six rows of pearls on gold wire and fastened with a gold catch.

'Perfect!' Tasnim declared. 'And now a ring.'

The ring he produced had a pearl the size of Tasmania, and Marni refused to even consider it, although a smaller ring, set with rows of seed pearls that went well with the bracelet, won her heart.

'Now that's enough,' she told Tasnim, but the woman was unstoppable. Ignoring Marni completely, she pulled out necklaces, bracelets and rings with stones that looked like emeralds and rubies. Studied them, then declared, 'No, we'll stick to sapphires because of your eyes, but now I am tired. Mazur, could you put together some sapphire sets and send them to my house?'

Mazur nodded, and followed the two of them out of the treasure trove, locking the door behind him before walking them out to the car. The driver held the door for Tasnim, while Mazur did the same for Marni, murmuring, as she slid past him, 'I am very happy for you and Prince Ghazi.' Marni sensed the kindly man actually meant it and immediately felt depressed.

She hadn't realised just how much she would hate deceiving people—maybe not people generally, but nice people like Mazur.

Fortunately Tasnim seemed to have finally run out of steam so the drive back to her home was quiet.

'I *will* rest now,' she said, 'but the driver will take you wherever you wish to go, or you can ask Shara for anything you need if you decide to stay in your room. The boutique will package up all we've bought and send it here, probably by later today, so you can choose what you want to wear to dinner tonight.'

'Dinner tonight?' Marni queried.

Tasnim smiled.

'Did I not tell you? Ghazi phoned to say he would pick you up at seven to take you out to dinner. It will be to somewhere special so—no, I won't let you decide. I'll come to your room later and we'll decide together what you will wear. Remember, this will be your first public appearance and although as yet your betrothal is not known, people will notice you and begin to talk.'

Marni's stomach knotted at the thought, but she *had* agreed and she'd gone along with the purchase of all the new clothes so she couldn't deny being aware that they would be needed.

'Okay,' she said, letting the word escape in a sigh.

But underneath her trepidation a bud of excitement began to unfurl.

She would be seeing Ghazi—how easy it was to think of him that way after being with Tasnim most of the day—tonight!

Which was really pathetic if she thought about it. This was all pretence!

CHAPTER SEVEN

THE EXCITEMENT HAD waned by the time she was dressed, waiting with Tasnim in the big room at the front of the house. Her own reflection, as well as Tasnim's cries of delight, had told her she looked good, but uneasiness boiled inside her.

This dressing up in clothes paid for by someone else seemed to underline the fact that it was all pretence, and the subterfuge made Marnie feel queasy. It was one thing to pretend for the sake of his sisters but for other people that she would surely meet, people who looked up to him as their ruler—was it right to be deceiving them?

'Ghazi will not be able to take his eyes off you,' Tasnim was saying, 'and how he'll keep his hands off you—whoo-hoo, it will be near impossible. Such fun!'

Considering her more personal reason for being in Ablezia, Marni would have liked to ask if

Ghazi would *have* to keep his hands off her, as Tasnim seemed to be intimating. But that question was far too personal—too fraught with hidden mines and traps to even consider asking.

Beside which, she was reasonably certain formal betrothals didn't include the couple going to bed together, while actually making love with the ruler of a country—any country—was so far beyond Marni's imagining it had to be impossible!

'The car is here!'

Tasnim's—was he a butler?—appeared, and made the announcement, then vanished in his usual silent way.

'Oh, bother Ghazi,' Tasnim muttered. 'He's sent a car, not come himself, and I did want to see his face when he saw you looking so beautiful.'

'It's just the clothes,' Marni told her, using words to hide the little stirring of disappointment at Gaz's non-arrival, and her embarrassment over Tasnim's praise.

'No, it is you,' Tasnim argued. 'Of course the clothes help, but you have a serenity about you that enhances whatever you are wearing, and that's part of true beauty.'

As if! her head mocked, but Tasnim's words helped ease Marni's disappointment, and she walked out to the car, slipped into the back seat and settled her beautiful new clothes around her.

Cinderella going to the ball, was her first thought, but if that had been the case she'd have been wearing one of the ballgowns.

And glass slippers!

She sighed and wondered just what lay ahead of her on this, the second momentous day in this new, and totally fantasy, life.

Lost in her thoughts and concerns over pretence, she barely noticed where the driver was taking her until she saw the palace looming up ahead.

'We're going to the palace?'

Duh!

'No, miss, we're going to Sheikh Nimr's home. His wife, Sheikha Alima, is preparing a special banquet in your honour.'

A special *banquet*! Great!

Fortunately Gaz was at the top of the steps as the vehicle pulled up and it was he who came down to open the car door for her, taking her hand to help her out, the light in his eyes as he took in her appearance enough, for a moment, to still her nerves.

'You are beautiful,' he murmured, for the second time that day.

'It's the clothes—the dressing up in this gorgeous gear—anyone would look beautiful,' she said, trying for lightness, although her fingers clung to his for support.

His smile told her he didn't agree, and it was the smile, plus the sensations firing through her that made her remove her hand and regain some common sense.

'A banquet?' she queried.

'Only a small one,' he assured her, smiling as she spoke. 'Having put all the sisters' noses out of joint by asking Tasnim if you could stay with her for a while, I have to start the conciliation process. Believe me, growing up with seven sisters is better training in diplomacy than any university degree.'

They had reached the top of the steps, and he paused, turning towards Marni to explain.

'I have to start with Alima because she is the

eldest. She has invited two other sisters, Meena and Ismah, and their husbands, as well as Nimr's brothers and their wives, the married ones. A small party and you do not have to remember everyone's names and if I don't get you inside very soon I shall have to kiss you right here and scandalise everyone.'

Marni had been trying to get her head around the names and wondering why only two sisters had been invited—with Tasnim she would now have met four of the seven—when Gaz—in a business suit so definitely Gaz—had added the last bit.

About the kiss...

So it wasn't *all* pretence...

Of course not, there's still the lust, she reminded herself, dousing her re-smouldering embers.

They paused at the front door, Marni preparing to slip off her sandals and noticing the ease with which Gaz removed his highly polished loafers.

'You learn our ways,' he said quietly.

'This one's easy,' Marni retorted, unsettled by the lust reminder as well as by his nearness.

The lust wasn't pretence.

Neither was it love!

But love's not been any part of this, the sensible part of Marni's brain responded.

And the funny lump of pain sneaked back into the middle of her chest.

'Have you an extremely tidy mind that you need to reposition your sandals three or four times, or are you having second thoughts about meeting the family?'

Gaz was waiting for her to move away from the neat array of sandals.

Marni pulled herself together and looked directly at him, hoping all her doubts and inner discussions weren't visible on her face.

'Only two of the other sisters?'

He smiled and her heart turned over.

Love not part of this?

'I'm breaking you in gently. I think you'll find Tasnim has already asked the others to lunch one day next week. Alima set the limits—ordered them all not to crowd you—and what Alima says goes with the women.'

He took her hand and placed it on his forearm, tucking her close to his side as they walked through the wide entranceway. Marni glimpsed the huge majlis off to the left, and was relieved when a white-clad servant bowed them into a smaller, though no less opulent room.

Where shades of yellow from palest lemon to deep, rich gold had been the dominant colours in the rooms Marni had seen in the palace, it was red that struck her here. Swathed red silk curtains framed arched openings into what appeared to be a courtyard garden, while deep vermilion couches were pushed back against the walls. The floor, again, was marble, but a creamy colour, streaked with red, so Marni wasn't surprised to find the woman walking towards her, hands outstretched in welcome, was also clad in what must be her favourite colour.

'My sister, Alima,' Gaz said smoothly. 'Alima, this is Marni.'

Alima clasped Marni's hands and drew her closer, kissing her on both cheeks—air kisses really, although the warmth of the woman's smile seemed genuine.

'What I wonder,' she declared as she looked Marni up and down, then down and up again, 'is how our father knew his son would be so difficult to please as far as women went, so he solved the problem early on, betrothing him to you.'

'I think it was probably a joke,' Marni said, the words popping out before she realised it was probably the wrong thing to say. But Alima was unfazed.

'My father *never* joked and, believe me, having cast upwards of a dozen beautiful and intelligent women in my brother's path over the years, I am more than ever convinced of my father's prescience.'

'You do rattle on,' Gaz said to his sister, but Marni heard fondness in his voice. 'Now, do your duty and introduce Marni around. I've told her she needn't remember all the names—in fact, any of them except for Meena and Ismah, and I assume you've seated her near them for dinner.'

Gaz—why when he was with Marni did he think of himself this way—watched Alima lead Marni into the throng, seeing the way the fluid material of her tunic swayed about her body, noticing the strands of fine silvery hair escaping from the dark blue shawl she'd draped over her head.

His silver wraith!

His body had tightened the moment she'd stepped out of the car, and he was sorry he'd chosen to wear a suit tonight. His kandora hid far more than trousers.

A string of oaths echoed through his head. He'd brought this on himself, betrothing himself to her, so if he wanted her, and he did, he'd better organise a wedding, and soon!

'Well chosen, brother!' He turned to find Nimr standing beside him. 'But you'd better secure her before my boys are old enough to challenge you. Karim is already in love with her—he talks of nothing but the soccer-playing blonde he found in the gardens.'

'Surely he's too young to be thinking of women,' Gaz protested, and Nimr laughed.

'Don't believe it for a minute. They mature early, our boys, and didn't we, as youngsters, believe an older woman could teach us much?'

Gaz laughed but he was looking around the room at the same time, and realised that not only were all four of his nephews included in the party—very smartly dressed in miniature suits—but Karim was right now chatting up Marni, making her laugh at something he'd said.

He's twelve, he reminded himself as he moved away from Nimr, easing his way through the crowd, hopefully unobtrusively but heading for his fiancée nonetheless.

'We'll have to lead the way into dinner,' he said when he arrived, taking Marni's arm in a possessive grasp. 'It's the way things are done.'

'Oh, but dinner won't be for ages,' Karim told him, 'and there must be people you have to see.'

'People Marni has to meet as well,' Gaz said firmly, at the same time telling himself he couldn't possibly be jealous of a twelve year old boy.

He was leading Marni towards Ismah's husband when two youngish men swerved into their path—Nimr's youngest brothers, unmarried as yet and more than a little wild. He introduced Marni and was pleased at their manners, although, as they moved away, Marni smiled and said, 'The wild ones of the family?'

The effect of the smile left him floundering to catch up with the question, and he had to find an echo of it in his head before it made sense.

'What makes you ask?'

Even that was a stalling tactic—he was still trying to come to grips with why a smile would stir his blood and have his body thinking about ravishment.

Marriage or distance—they were the only two options—and hadn't he promised he wouldn't rush her into marriage?

Well, not actually promised…

Although marriage hadn't been an issue when he'd asked her to pretend to the betrothal!

'They look like young men who are constantly seeking amusement—the kind that usually leads to trouble. I've met young men like them staying as guests at the hotel, young men with too much money and too much time on their hands, always looking for what they call fun but which often translates into something illegal.'

He heard the words but his mind was still following his body down the sex trail so he took little notice, although the word 'hotel' registered enough to give him the glimmer of an idea.

'Will you give me your grandfather's phone number? I should have asked before. I must phone him to—'

Marni giggled.

'To ask for my hand in marriage? Oh, really, Gaz! That is so old-fashioned. Besides, he is in hospital. Nelson emailed this afternoon to say the operation will be within the next few days.'

The giggle—such an inconsequential thing—had further activated the inappropriate desire he was feeling, but the idea was even better now. Out there, in Australia, anything might happen...

'Then we should fly out right away. You will want to be there when he has the operation and I can stay in the hotel so I don't put your Mr Nelson out at all.'

Pale eyes looked up at him, no mirth in them now, only fear and sorrow.

'He definitely doesn't want me there, Gaz,' she said softly. 'That's the main reason I'm over here. He's a proud man and doesn't want me to see him all weak and tied to tubes in the ICU, or have me

around while he's recovering. I promised him I'd
stay away.'

'But you'll be riven with worry and concern
and feel helpless because you're so far away.'

She tried a smile but it wavered with apprehen-
sion and he wondered if the response that burned
through his body might not be more than lust.

'I'll just have to deal with it, won't I?' she said,
the smile getting better. 'I promised! Besides, I'd
be just as helpless there! I know he's in the best
possible hands.'

'Ghazi, you must not monopolise your betrothed in this manner!'

Alima had appeared and before he could object, she whisked Marni away.

He'd drive her back to Tasnim's later! At least
that way they could kiss.

But wouldn't kisses make the longing worse,
the desire stronger?

Maybe putting some distance between them
would be better...

Marni allowed herself to be led through the
crowd, introduced to this one and that, realising
Gaz had been right, she'd *never* remember all the

names. Meena would be easy. She was very like Tasnim in looks.

'We are full sisters,' the pretty woman explained, 'the daughters of our father's third wife, the one before Ghazi's mother.'

'I was just thinking I'll never remember everyone's names and now you're making me realise I'll have to remember relationships as well.'

Meena touched her softly on the arm.

'Do not worry. It will come to you in time. For the moment, it is more than enough for us all that Ghazi is happy—that he has found the right woman to love.'

The 'love' word had its almost predictable effect in Marni's chest, but she was getting used to it so ignored it, reminding Meena instead that it wasn't love but an arrangement made by her father.

'Ah, but the old ones know,' Meena said. 'My marriage was arranged but when I met my husband I knew my father had been right for there was no one else in the world I could love as much.'

Intrigued by a culture so different from her

own, Marni couldn't help asking, 'Were all your marriages arranged?'

The question was probably too personal but Meena didn't seem to mind.

'Not really, although when Alima was about eight she decided she was going to marry Nimr, so then our father and our uncle betrothed them. Ismah met her husband at university in America. He is from a neighbouring country and will one day rule it so our father couldn't object to him. Tasnim, of course, just told our father she was going to marry Yusef and no one could ever argue with Tasnim.'

'I can understand that,' Marni put in, but if Meena heard her she didn't show it, continuing on down or up the family tree.

'Our other sisters, well, you'll meet them eventually, but Zahrah is married to a Westerner, the son of one of our father's old friends and advisors, Maryam is married to her work, she is a doctor like Ghazi, and Rukan is married to another of our cousins. They were both betrothed to others but ran away to get married and our father forgave them both because they were obviously meant for each other.'

Just as Marni decided it would be impossible to remember even the sisters' names, Alima rescued her, taking her off to meet other guests, including Ismah, a slight, plump woman with such beautiful eyes Marni could barely stop staring at her.

'She is beautiful, yes?' the man beside Ismah said, and Marni could only nod and smile.

'As are you,' Ismah said quietly, and Marni shook her head. Among these exotically beautiful women she faded into oblivion.

Gaz returned to lead her into dinner, explaining on the way that although all those present were family, the women would still sit together at one end of the table and the men at the other.

Marni smiled at him.

'Sounds like an Aussie barbeque,' she said. 'The men in one group the women in another.'

'Here it makes sense as most of the women live with their husbands, so at gatherings like this they enjoy gossiping with the other women, and the men enjoy catching up on politics or, more likely, the latest football scores and transfers.'

'*Most* of the women live with their husbands?'

His turn to smile.

'As against the old days when they would all have lived in the harem, visiting their husband in his tent, or later his palace, when invited.'

The teasing glint in his eyes made Marni's insides flutter. What had she got herself into, and where was this going?

Had he read the questions in her eyes that he gave her hand, where it rested on his arm, a slight squeeze before abandoning her to his sisters at the women's end of the table?

To Marni's great relief the meal was not a banquet in the true sense of the word, with endless plates of food laid out in the middle of the table. Instead, light-footed serving women offered plates of this and that, placing small or large spoonfuls of each dish directly onto the guests' plates.

And contrary to her impression that personal conversation was off limits in this country, she was peppered with questions about herself, her home and her family.

'We all remember that visit to the beautiful

hotel,' Ismah told her. 'Alima and Rukan were betrothed already, but Maryam and Meena flirted shamelessly with the young man who worked on the concierge desk, flashing their eyes at him and teasing him so he blushed whenever one of us came near, because he couldn't really tell us apart.'

'You flirted too,' Meena reminded her. 'And remember the day Zahrah went out without her abaya, in Western jeans and a T-shirt and her hair in a ponytail for everyone to see.'

The sisters laughed.

'Oh, I remember that,' Alima said. 'She went to Sea World to ride on the big roller-coaster and she was so sick she had to ring the hotel and ask them to send a car to take her back there.'

'And Father said she'd shamed the family and would never get a husband.'

'That's probably why he sent her to America,' Meena said, and the women laughed, as if that had been a good thing, not a punishment.

The talk turned to other holidays, other places all the women had stayed at one time or another, London and Berlin apparently favourites with them all. Sitting listening to them, Marni realised how at ease with each other they all were, even the women married to Nimr's brothers.

Was this normal in all families?

Not having one—not an extended one—she couldn't judge, but their obvious closeness once again reminded her that her position was a false one, and the niggle of disquiet that rarely left her these days began to make itself felt more persistently.

'I will drive you home.'

Gaz appeared at her side as the women left the dining room. He took her hand once again and placed it on his arm in the formal manner he had used before.

She said goodbye to the women she had met, sought out Alima to thank her for the evening, then let Gaz guide her to the door, exhaustion nipping at her heels as the tension she hadn't realised she'd been feeling drained from her.

Pausing at the front door, she managed to get one sandal on but was having trouble with the second when Gaz knelt and slipped it on her foot.

'Oh, no!' she protested, not sure whether to laugh or cry, 'that is just far *too* Cinderella! Is your car a pumpkin?'

He looked at her, bemused, but at least it gave her something to talk to him about, explaining the story of Cinderella and her prince.

'They were real, these people?' he asked, driving through night-quiet streets, the engine in the big saloon purring quietly in the background.

'No, it's a children's fairy-tale,' Marni told him. 'It's just that I can't help thinking of it.' She paused, then added quietly, 'Probably because it's easier to be thinking of my life right now as a fairy-tale than be worrying over deceiving nice people like your sisters and their friends.'

He had pulled the car over as she was talking and she looked around, seeing a long wall with an arched opening in it, an ornate gate protecting whatever lay behind the walls.

'You have the photo,' he said, turning and taking both her hands in his. 'How is there deceit?'

'It's pretence—you asked me to pretend, remember, to get your sisters off your back.'

'And it is working,' he said, lifting her hands

and kissing the backs of her fingers, one by one, so she had to struggle to keep her brain working while her body melted from something as unsexy as finger kisses. 'So much so they are asking about the wedding—about when it will be.'

If finger kisses had melted her bones, talk of a wedding sent such heat washing through her she could barely breathe.

Had to breathe!

Had to protest.

'But we're doing this to give you time to get to know your job,' she reminded him, hoping he wouldn't hear just how shaky her voice was. 'A wedding, even if we wanted to marry—well, the kind of fuss that would surely entail would interrupt your schedule far more than just being betrothed. It would be a terrible distraction.'

He didn't reply, simply using his grasp on her hands to draw her closer then dropping his head to kiss her on the lips.

'This particular distraction,' he said a long time later, tilting her head so he could look into her eyes, 'is interrupting my schedule more than you could ever know. If we were married there'd be *one* distraction less.'

She frowned at him.

'Are you talking about sex? Is that the distraction that's so hard to handle?'

He kissed her again, but lightly.

'Do you not find it so?' he teased, and just as she was about to admit she felt it, too, she remembered the virginity thing and was flooded with embarrassment.

Should she tell him now?

But how?

What would he think?

That she was frigid, or had something wrong with her?

Or decide she was pathetic, locked in adolescence, as the last man she'd dated had. Christmas cake, he'd called her, apparently a foreign insult for an older virgin, dried out the way a cake did after the twenty-fifth of December.

He'd laughed at the notion that there was anything special about virginity—not that she'd considered it that way. As far as he'd been concerned, it was nothing more than an embarrassing nuisance. Men, he'd told her, expected a woman to have had experience and be able to please a man in bed.

And that had been a man she'd thought she loved!

The thought of telling Gaz—of his reaction— made her tremble. It was one thing to think she could tell some man with whom she was having a virginity-relieving fling about it, but telling Gaz?

'I think we'd better just stay betrothed,' she muttered, her voice sounding like a very creaky gate in desperate need of oil.

CHAPTER EIGHT

'ARE YOU TIRED, or would you walk with me a little way?

Marni, who'd been expecting an argument, or at least further discussion, over the marriage business, was startled.

'Walk?

'In the oasis,' Gaz said, waving a hand towards the gate. 'Have you been there?'

'I remember going past the wall on my way somewhere, but haven't been inside it. Won't it be dark?'

'Wait and see,' Gaz said. He was already opening his door, coming around to open hers and offering his hand to help her out.

He led her to the gate and unlatched it, ushering her inside onto a path between what seemed like a jungle of palm trees. The path was lit by lampposts placed at intervals, and the palms were lit from below by soft floodlights.

'It's like an enchanted forest,' she whispered as they walked through shadows.

'It has been here for thousands of years,' Gaz explained. 'There is a spring, and our ancestors built a series of narrow canals out from it so the palms would thrive. It is here for all our people to enjoy, and the dates are free to anyone who wishes to pick one or many.'

The soft air smelled sweet, and a slight breeze ruffled the fringed palm leaves, so it seemed as if they walked through a world apart.

'Will you pick one?' Marni asked, enjoying the sight of the palms growing so closely, and the little paths that led this way and that but still wondering what they were doing here, given the late hour and the marriage conversation, which seemed to have been forgotten.

'Of course, that is why we are here.'

He held her hand and was leading her to the right then to the left, taking paths seemingly at random. Yet when he answered, she'd heard something in his voice—something that was Ghazi, not Gaz. This place must be special to him—like the desert—part of who he was…

Why?

'Dates and camels, these have kept my people alive down through the ages,' he said quietly, apparently answering her unspoken question. 'The date is especially miraculous as it can be eaten fresh, or dried and kept for months while the tribes travelled across the desert. The pulp makes sweets and bread, the seeds can be ground for flour, the fibrous mass that holds the dates is used for brooms, the palm leaves for thatch. But it is the legend that brings us here tonight.'

'A legend?'

'A story like your Cinderella. You reminded me of it when you told me your fairy-tale. The date grove is the one place a betrothed couple may walk together without a chaperone.'

Marni looked around and smiled.

'I can understand that—they can hardly get up to much with the narrow pathways and the little canals and the prickly fronds of the date palms pressing in on all sides.'

'Ah, but they walk together for a reason,' Ghazi said, stopping by a heavy cluster of ripening dates drooping from a palm. 'Our legend says if they find the perfect date, ripe and ready to eat, and they feed it to each other, not only will their marriage be fertile but they will live long together.'

'Just live?' Marni queried. She knew she should be protesting the marriage thing again, yet here she was querying a single word.

Had she been hoping the legend would say live and love?

Of course she had! It was the silly lump that kept forming in her chest causing this sudden longing for—

Love? Get over it, Marni! Love was never the issue here! It's the marriage thing you should be worrying about!

She knew he was talking marriage now so they could go to bed together—a marriage dictated by lust. Although she hadn't seen much of her mother since she'd abandoned her daughter to Pop and Nelson, she had memories of her mother's desperate search for love, and understood now how lust could be mistaken for it.

Did she want that?

No!

'Of course live,' Ghazi said, his attention still on the cluster of dates. 'Aha! I have it.'

He plucked a date and turned towards her, holding it to her lips so she could take a bite.

'Just a bite,' he warned. 'You must then feed me.'

Ghazi was watching her, his eyes intent, his fingers moving closer to her lips.

It's only a legend, she told herself, but her heart was pounding and suddenly being fed a date—well, half a date—by this man was the most erotic thing that had ever happened to her.

Her body afire, she opened her lips and bit into the sweet, juicy flesh. Ghazi's thumb brushed her lower lip and she felt her nipples peak beneath her tunic and a near orgasmic heat between her thighs.

'Now you,' he said, his voice so husky it rasped against her sensitised skin.

He handed her the date and she lifted it towards his lips, her fingers trembling as he opened his mouth and his even white teeth bit into it, taking it and her finger and thumb into the moist cavern of his mouth, suckling at them while her body pulsed with need.

He released her fingers, disposed of the seed then drew her close so they embraced within the heady scent of the dates, and her body pressed against his, feeling his reaction to the tasting, wanting him so badly she was beyond all rational thought.

Never had he held such a responsive woman in his arms—never felt a need that matched his own in its ferocity, and he'd gone and betrothed himself to her and so put her off limits for the moment. He could not tarnish her name with his family or his people by sneaking in or out of lodgings or hotels, and both the palace and Tasnim's place were off limits for the same reason.

He could kiss her, but kisses made things worse—but he couldn't not kiss her...

Ghazi groaned and held her more tightly, pressing the softness of her body against his, fitting the two halves that were man and woman together to make a whole, aware she must know just how much he wanted her.

'It's like a madness, my desire for you,' he

whispered, before his lips closed on hers, seeking to devour her, to draw her body into his, to make her his for ever.

For ever?

The words echoed in his head.

Surely he didn't mean it.

Yes, he desired her, and would marry her if only to assuage that desire, but such desire—lust even—did not last for ever. He knew that from experience. Marriage, then a suitable arrangement to end it and no one any the worse off. Marni, in fact, would be better off, although he was aware her grandfather must be a wealthy man. But her settlement would certainly include a house and enough money to live on without having to work—she'd take whatever jewels he gave her during the marriage, it would all be worked out by his advisors and—

She was pulling away from him, peering up at his face as if to read it in the shadows.

'You're not with me in this kiss, are you?' she asked. 'I think it best you take me back to Tasnim's.'

He didn't argue, couldn't, yet as he walked with

her, back the way they'd come, he felt a sense of loss—not for the kiss, there'd be other kisses, but because of the conclusions he had reached.

Although they had to be the correct ones, the best for both of them, surely…

Tasnim had been in bed when Marni had returned the previous evening, but Shara had been waiting up for her and Marni had asked the young woman to wake her for breakfast in time for her to get to the hospital to do her shift.

She didn't know what Gaz might have arranged at the hospital, but she was due on duty and she'd decided that was where she most wanted to be. At least there she could concentrate on work and forget all the mind-boggling stuff going on in the rest of her life here in Ablezia, as well as her worries over Pop's imminent operation.

So, early next morning, reminding Shara to explain to Tasnim, Marni went out to the car Shara had arranged for her, feeling like her real self in her uniform and hospital shoes.

Cinderella back in the kitchen after the ball!

Jawa was surprised to see her, yet pleased.

'As far as we know, there's been no change in our work schedules so if you hadn't turned up we'd have been a nurse short. We're in Theatre Three with the Frenchman for the morning, then with a paediatric orthopaedic surgeon this afternoon.

'Good. We should be busy,' Marni said, knowing she needed something—anything—to distract herself from thoughts of Pop.

And Gaz!

And *marriage,* whatever that might have meant…

Not to mention memories of the last time she'd told a man she was a virgin…

Work went well, and Marni enjoyed the sense of teamwork that was typical of operating theatres—the moments of drama, the excitement when a tricky bit of cutting or stitching was successful, the quiet pleasure when a job was done.

As they finished their shift, she and Jawa left the changing rooms together.

'Coffee?' Jawa asked, but Marni shook her head.

'I want to sit with Safi for a while. I've been neglecting him lately.'

It was mostly true, but when she'd checked her phone for messages earlier she'd found a text from Nelson telling her Pop's operation was going ahead that day.

Working out the time difference, she knew he'd be in Theatre right now, and although she knew worrying about it was pointless she couldn't help feeling anxious, tense and sick-to-her-stomach nervous. Neither did she want to return to her current abode and have to explain her concerns or distraction to the ever-bubbly Tasnim.

'So I'm really hiding here,' she said to Safi when she entered his room and settled by his bed, taking his hand in hers. She knew he didn't understand her but the slight pressure of his thin fingers told her he was glad she was there.

She sang the songs she knew he liked and watched him drift off to sleep, before picking up his chart and checking what had been going on with him.

As far as she could see, he was doing well.

Pop would be, too! If she couldn't be there, the

least she could do was send positive thoughts in his direction.

You *will* get through it! You *will* be well!

'I thought I'd find you here. Tasnim phoned to say you'd sent the driver home and would take a taxi later. Drivers will always wait, you know.'

Marni smiled up at the man who'd entered the room so silently he'd been standing beside her before she realised it.

And before her body reacted?

She *must* be distracted!

'No, I didn't know that,' she said, trying for lightness, although she felt strangely intimidated by the white-robed Ghazi.

'Is it your grandfather?' he asked, pulling over a chair and sitting beside her, taking her free hand in his so the three of them were linked.

Marni nodded.

'He's in Theatre now.'

Had he felt a tremor in her hand that his fingers tightened on hers?

'I could organise a hook-up to the hospital so you know exactly what's going on,' he offered, rubbing his thumb back and forth across the palm of her hand—distracting her in spite of her concern.

'Nelson has promised to contact me when it's over and he's spoken to the surgeon,' she said, turning to look at him, reading his sympathy in his dark eyes, feeling weakness all through her that this man should care enough to be here for her.

Not that she could let him see her reaction. He was being practical—sensible—and she could do both!

'I know the routine of the op, and that makes it both easier and harder,' she said. 'They'll open his chest and bypass the two stents in his coronary arteries before opening his heart to replace the valve.'

'You've seen the operation before?'

'I worked in the cardiac theatre for a while when I was training. It's a long, hard operation, but generally there aren't too many risks.'

Ghazi took both her hands now and smiled gently at her.

'Or so you keep telling yourself,' he said. 'Now come, you need to eat. We'll go to the restaurant at the top of the building again. You can turn your phone back on up there and be ready when your Mr Nelson calls.'

Marni stared at him, feeling a frown forming between her eyebrows.

'But you've no time for this,' she protested. 'You said yourself you've got a schedule from hell and I've already taken up too much of your time. I'll just sit here for a while then go on back to Tasnim's—even phone her to send a driver if that will make you happy.'

His smile was broader this time, and it started up all the reactions her preoccupation had held at bay.

'If the country's boss can't take time out to be with his betrothed when she needs him, who can? Besides, the dinner I was meant to be attending promised to be boring in the extreme—a meeting of some world soccer association organised by Nimr—and the men attending won't know one sheikh from another. To them we're all just men in long white dresses—so one less will hardly matter.'

Still holding her hands, he eased her gently

to her feet, but before he left the room, he, too, looked at Safi's chart and examined the little boy who lay sleeping quietly in the big bed.

'He seems to be doing well,' Marni said, as they walked towards the lifts.

But Ghazi's, 'Yes,' was distracted.

'You're worried about him?' she asked as they waited in the foyer.

'Worried about his family situation,' Ghazi admitted. 'I really don't want to send him home while he recovers enough for another operation, but he's already been away from home for a month and that's a long time for a child. Also, he can't stay at the hospital. I can keep him at the palace, of course. The women would look after him and there are children he can play with, but his family—'

The lift doors opened in front of them and they stepped in, the three occupants inside nodding their heads towards Ghazi, while Marni considered the conversation they'd just had.

This man was the ruler of his nation, battling to come to terms with his 'job' and to meet the demands made of him, yet he had time to worry over one small boy, or made time to worry about him.

He was special—not the boy but the man! The realisation wasn't a total shock—Ghazi had shown his empathy with people before, his being here with her tonight being one example—but…

The warmth unfolding in her chest as she pondered these things was different—not lust at all!

Oh, surely not the other 'l' word,' she thought as they left the lift and a warm hand on her back, guiding her towards the restaurant, sparked her more recognisable reactions. To fall in love with this man would be madness! They were from different worlds, so different she doubted any marriage could survive, especially if the love was one-sided.

He'd spoken the truth when he'd said he wouldn't be missed at the sports dinner, Ghazi mused as he asked the waiter for a table overlooking the desert, but there'd been many other things he could have been doing.

So why was he here?

Kindness—Marni was a stranger in his land and at the moment needed some support.

Right! said the cynic within him. You couldn't have made sure Tasnim or one of your other sisters was with her?

And was support the only reason you wanted to be with her?

Honesty compelled him to admit it wasn't.

He'd *wanted* to see her.

Needed to see her!

Not only to see her but to touch her, even just minimally as touches must be in public.

This was crazy!

This was a betrothal of convenience and somehow he'd allowed himself to become attracted to the woman.

Allowed?

Did one *allow* such reactions to happen, or were they beyond human control?

Surely not! He'd always been able to control such impulses before.

'Sir?'

The waiter had obviously asked him a question as both he and Marni were looking at him, obviously puzzled.

'Sorry!'

He dragged his mind back to the present. This was hardly the time to be questioning his behaviour.

'This time you will choose what we eat,' he said to Marni. 'There is an explanation for all the dishes in English, so you decide.'

He smiled, hoping she'd forget his distraction.

Some hope! She'd no sooner finished ordering and the waiter had disappeared than she asked, 'Are you worried about something? Is it still Safi or was it more important than you made out, this dinner you're missing? Because if it is, or if there's something else you should be doing, I'll be fine on my own. I could even go to Jawa's rooms and wait for the phone call there. She'd understand.'

He gazed at the woman across the table from him, aware how worried she must be beneath her cool exterior, yet here she was worrying about *him*! When had anyone last concerned themselves about his welfare—apart from Mazur and a couple of his closest servants?

She disturbed him in ways apart from the purely physical...

'Ghazi?'

His name, softly spoken, reminded him she'd asked a question and deserved a reply. But there was more—the name itself—more internal disturbance.

'That is the first time you've used my full name,' he said, reaching out across the table to touch her hand where it rested beside her water glass.

Her smile stirred the more usual disturbances.

'That's because when you're in your prince gear I can't help but think of you as Ghazi. Gaz is just a bloke—an Aussie term for an ordinary man—but in that get-up you have to be Ghazi.'

She paused then added, 'But don't think you've distracted me with this talk of names. You're obviously worried about something and if it's that I'm keeping you from where you should be, please believe I'll be okay on my own.'

He had to smile.

'I know you would. I am coming to realise just how strong and capable my betrothed is, but I want to be with you tonight.' It was his turn to pause, though what he added was, 'In many ways,' which made the colour rise in her cheeks and his own body harden.

Fortunately their dinner arrived, the waiter setting down plates and different dishes in the middle of the table, offering them first to Marni, who had chosen them.

They ate, and talked of food, but he could see her anxiety growing, and noticed the quick glances she was giving her watch.

'Come,' he said, 'we can get a snack at Tasnim's later if we're hungry, but for now we'd be better waiting somewhere quiet. I've an office here, on the floor below. I'll order some coffee and sweetmeats to be sent there and we can both be comfortable.'

The relief on her face told him he'd made the right decision, and although she smiled her thanks as she pushed back her chair and stood up, he knew all she wanted to do was be somewhere private when she heard the results of the operation.

He distanced himself when the phone rang, standing by the windows while she burrowed deep into one of his armchairs, the hand that held the tiny mobile to her ear trembling slightly.

He only heard her end of the conversation but could tell from the relaxation in her voice that all had gone well, so he was surprised when she'd said goodbye to turn and see the tears trickling down her cheeks.

'Marni? It's all right, isn't it? I heard you saying "That's good" all the time. I realise it will be a while before he's out of the CCU but your grandfather's come through it well, hasn't he?'

Marni scrubbed at her cheeks, ashamed of her tears when everything had gone well. Far better than the surgeon had expected, according to Nelson.

'Are they tears of relief?' Ghazi asked.

He'd taken off his headdress and come to sit on the arm of her chair, his hand resting gently on her shoulder.

'Mostly relief, I suppose,' she admitted. 'I'm sorry to be such a wuss, but when Nelson said goodbye he called me "darling girl". Nelson hasn't called me that for years and I guess it just broke me up.'

'Darling girl! What a lovely phrase. He's something special, the man called Nelson.'

'He is indeed,' Marni responded, resting her head against Ghazi's side and remembering just how special Nelson had always been to her. 'Pop was very good with children but once they started to grow up, girls especially, he became…not embarrassed but less approachable somehow.

'He always blamed himself for how my mother turned out, always seeking love in the wrong places. So it was Nelson who had to check I knew about the birds and the bees—he actually used those words—and he'd call me darling girl when he talked about growing up, and give me little lectures about believing in myself, and about honour and respect and loyalty—all the things he felt were most important in the way we live our lives, all the things Pop lived by but couldn't put into words.'

She looked up at the man she'd been leaning on, suddenly embarrassed by all she'd revealed.

'Not that you need to know all that! It's just the words brought it all back. I'm sorry. You've already been so good, and here I am babbling on about Nelson bringing me up.'

The dark eyes were unfathomable, but as he moved she sensed what was coming and her body tightened as he dipped his head and kissed her on the lips.

'I think I owe your Nelson a big favour,' he said quietly, breathing the words against her skin, then his lips returned to hers and the kiss deepened, taking her away from the past and the present, to where sensation swamped all thoughts.

CHAPTER NINE

COULD SHE BLAME the relief that had set in after talking to Nelson, or was it just that this man had been so good, so kind and considerate, so *there* for her, that her response was so heated when he kissed her the second time?

Somehow, as the kiss deepened, they'd moved, Ghazi in the chair, she mostly on top of him, her arms wound around his neck, her body snuggling against his.

His hands were on her breasts, brushing across them, teasing them to a heavy longing, while his lips explored her face, kisses brushing eyelids, temple, the little hollow beneath her chin.

Her hands explored his back, feeling the hard muscle beneath the white robe, and ranged across his head, his beautifully shaped head, dark hair cut close to the scalp, her fingers teasing at his ears, wanting more contact with his skin.

Now his lips found hers again, deep, drugging kisses, while his hands travelled lower, fingers seeking sensitive parts while she squirmed against his hardness and wanted more and more of him, wanted the feel of his skin on hers, wanted to know him by touch, to tease him as he was teasing her.

Could she?

Awareness that she had never felt this way before—had never known she could—was somewhere in her consciousness, but buried deeply beneath the sensations she was experiencing.

The sensations she was enjoying!

Inflamed by his fingers, trembling on the brink, she heard him saying something but the words didn't penetrate the fog of longing enveloping both her body and her brain.

She moved and felt a shudder of release, a promise of things to come that she didn't fully understand but knew she wanted.

Her excitement must have stirred more arousal in him, for now they were joined in a macabre dance as they tried to strip each other's clothes off, while still kissing, still touching, still stoking the fires in both their bodies.

'There's a couch, for emergency overnight stays,' Ghazi said, half leading her, half carrying her towards an open door at the side of the office.

She glimpsed a small bathroom then an even smaller room, as plain as a monk's cell, one narrow bed against the wall, but Ghazi had stripped off his robe and stood before her, a snowy-white sarong tied around his waist—untied now, the full magnificence of the man revealed.

Her lungs jammed, she couldn't breathe—had to—

He drew her close, her trousers and tunic gone, her bra disposed of next, his lips suckling on her breast, her body in a torment of need as his fingers slipped beneath her knickers, touching her already sensitised nub, and she knew the little whimpering noises were coming from her, although an occasional groan suggested he was as aroused as she was.

Now on the bed, his fingers inside her, feeling the hardness of him against her soft abdomen, need outweighing any lingering doubt she might have had—need, and fear that he'd stop if she admitted—

He mustn't rush! Ghazi told himself.

How could he not?

Control was about the last thing on his mind now this woman who'd been driving him insane with desire was finally naked beneath, or nearly beneath him.

Yet he wanted to savour this first experience of the two of them together, for her sake as much as for his, and the way he felt now he'd be rushing towards a finish like an adolescent boy!

He cupped her flushed cheeks in his hands and pressed a kiss on her lips, slowing himself down, breathing deeply, allowing her time to…

To say no?

Could he stand it?

He didn't have to—not if the way she was returning his kiss was any indication. The kiss was surely her answer to his unspoken question, a kiss that burned along his nerves while her fingers teased his skin, trailing across his abdomen, his chest, brushing against his nipples.

He knelt above her, pressing kisses on her pale skin, sliding his tongue across her nipples while she squirmed beneath the attention, her breath rasping in her throat.

Trailing kisses down her chest, he teased her belly button with his tongue. Her hands were on his head, half holding him back, half urging him on.

He kissed her lower, felt a flinch of uncertainty and returned to use his lips and tongue in torment on her breasts while his fingers did the exploration.

He felt her tightness, warmth and slickness—heat—felt a tremble that told him she was ready, more than ready, her response to his attentions exciting him beyond reason—beyond control.

He took her hand and cupped it around his length, urging her to guide him in. Her fingers were shaking, and he slid his hands beneath her buttocks, easing her off the bed so he could slide inside that hot, moist sheath.

Slide inside now in one quick thrust, the idea of not rushing forgotten in his need to take her, make her his, and himself hers in the give and take of sexual pleasure.

Her fingers slipped away, he thrust again, heard her cry out but it was too late—far too late— her movement beneath him driving him on. Her cries were different now, asking for more, need- ing more, seeking her satisfaction as well as his.

Her body gripped him, her legs lifted to link around his back, they moved as one until he burst apart, collapsing on her, feeling the quivers in her body that told him she had found her own plea- sure and release.

But as common sense returned he realised what had happened and anger surged through him— anger at himself.

He'd taken advantage of this woman at a time when she was most vulnerable, comforting her with kisses that had led to this, never for a min- ute dreaming she might be a virgin. Then he'd let the desire he'd held in check since he'd first met her take over, when he should have—

Well, there was a lot he should have done.

Al'ana! How was he to know? Women her age…

He heaved himself away from her, sat up on the very edge of the narrow bed, his back to her, searching for something to say.

'You should have told me,' he finally managed, then realised the words had come out as an accusation, not an excuse.

He felt her move behind him and watched as she slid off the bed, briskly gathering up her discarded clothing, her beautiful, slim body silvered by the moonlight through the window.

His body stirred again, almost ready, but she'd straightened now and faced him.

'And have you ridicule me?' she demanded angrily. 'Tell me men expect women of my age to be more experienced? Tell me you're beyond wanting to teach a virgin about sex? I wanted it as much as you did, and I'm sorry if I disappointed you. Now, I'm going to have a shower and get dressed and I'd be grateful if you'd call a driver to take me back to Tasnim's.'

He sat on the bed as the bathroom door closed behind her, trying to make sense of the situation. First the virgin thing, then the things she'd said—she'd been *mocked* because of it?

How hurtful!

How damaging to her.

And now *he'd* made things worse.

Or he thought he probably had.

Seven sisters and he didn't have any understanding whatsoever of women and the stuff that went on in their heads.

Seduced by tears in grey-blue eyes and lips as soft as rose petals, he'd done the one thing he'd been determined not to do—made love to Marni.

And having had her once…

It didn't bear thinking about, but he did know he couldn't sit in the back of a dimly lit limousine with her while his driver took her home.

He picked up the phone and asked Tasnim's major domo to send a car to meet Marni at the entrance to the hospital, but his phone call alerted someone to where he was, because now the phone was ringing, Mazur asking him if he could call in at Nimr's dinner on his way home. He was arguing about the uselessness of that as Marni slipped out of the bathroom, nodded once in his direction then headed out through his office towards the door.

'Wait, I'll walk you to the car,' he called, while Mazur listed reasons he should do this one thing for his cousin.

Marni turned then shook her head and disappeared from view.

Lost in thoughts of what might have been, of should she have done it or shouldn't she, and all the other questions that had arisen out of their coupling, it took Marni a while to realise the car she was entering already had a passenger.

'Are you all right?' Tasnim asked. 'I know you phoned earlier to say you'd be late home, but I was a little worried, so when Hari, Nimr's youngest brother, who was visiting, offered to come and collect you, I came along as well.'

Marni took her hand and squeezed her fingers.

'You are far too kind to me,' she said. 'I visited Safi, the little boy I've told you about, then Ghazi kindly said I could wait for my phone call from home in his office.'

'Your grandfather's operation? It was today? It went well?'

'Yes, and, yes, and, yes,' Marni said, and for a moment in her pleasure and relief at being able to report that she forgot what had happened after the phone call.

But only for a moment.

What on earth must Ghazi think of her?

How could she have been so stupid as to think it would all be okay?

'What was that?'

She turned to Tasnim, aware the other woman had said something—had sounded concerned.

'We're going the wrong way,' Tasnim repeated, pointing out towards the road.

'I can't help you but surely Hari knows the way. Ask him.'

She hoped she didn't sound as distracted as she felt. As far as she was concerned, Hari could take her out into the desert and drop her there.

Tasnim rapped on the glass that separated the passengers from the driver but when Hari didn't turn, she picked up the handpiece for the intercom, talking into it, then yelling into it.

He didn't answer.

'The wretched boy! I don't know why I agreed to let him drive us tonight. It's just that his brother's away somewhere—Fawzi, the other young one he hangs around with—and I thought he must be lonely to have come for a visit. Then when he wanted to play chauffeur I went along with it. This will be some bet they've had, or some daft joke they've dreamed up. The two of them are always up to something.'

Tasnim was sounding angry and concerned enough to distract Marni from her morbid thoughts.

'Can you phone your home? Tell someone what's happening?' Marni asked.

Tasnim shook her head.

'I was only coming for the ride to collect you. I didn't think to bring my mobile. But you'd have yours.'

Marni felt around her on the seat then remembered Hari—only she hadn't realised it was Hari—taking her handbag as she'd got into the car. He'd put it on the front seat—behind that nice, impenetrable barrier.

A smidgen of concern sneaked into her already tortured thoughts but considering Tasnim's condition, surely it was best to pretend that it was all some kind of joke.

'Well, as there's nothing we can do, we'll have to relax and go along with it,' Marni said, almost pleased to have something other than Ghazi to consider. 'Think of the baby and don't let yourself get upset.'

'Don't let myself get upset? It's ten o'clock at night and I'm usually in bed by nine these days. I was only up because Hari was there and he seemed to want company.'

Tasnim's voice was becoming more and more strident, and concern for her and her unborn child soon outweighed Marni's guilt and anxiety over what had just happened with Ghazi.

'Breathe deeply,' she told Tasnim. 'Calm yourself down. We're in the car, we're safe, and we really can't do anything other than sit back, relax and wait to see what happens.'

'I'll kill him!' Tasnim declared, leaning forward so she could hammer on the heavy screen.

'Later!' Marni said, capturing Tasnim's hands and massaging them, forcing her to lie back against the seat, talking quietly until the distressed woman calmed down.

Forget the joke, Marni now felt almost as much

anger and murderous intent towards Hari but she kept it hidden, knowing the most important thing was to keep Tasnim as calm as possible. Eight months into her first pregnancy, a bout of hysterics was the last thing she needed.

'We're out on the desert road,' Tasnim told her, and Marni looked out the car windows, surprised to see the city must be far behind them for there was nothing as far as she could see—well, nothing but the dunes and sand, lit by the headlights as the car raced up the broad highway.

'It's the road to the old palace. That's Hari's joke. He's taking us to join the harem—he probably thinks that's where all the women should be.'

The idea that they were going somewhere specific seemed to calm Tasnim and she rested her head back against the seat, wriggled around to get comfortable, and promptly fell asleep.

Leaving Marni alone with nothing but her memories of what had happened before she'd left the hospital—memories she didn't want, things she most definitely didn't want to think about.

She thought of Pop instead, of how he must be feeling, picturing him in the CCU, all wired up to machines, tubes anchoring him to his bed. How he'd hate it, being so helpless, so reliant on others. Hopefully he wouldn't be conscious enough to be aware of it.

Her heart ached for him, but Nelson would be there…

The car stopped, but definitely not at any palace for, looking around, Marni could see nothing but desert and more desert, and perhaps a cloud of dust, just visible in the distance, gradually revealing another vehicle as it came into the beams of the headlights.

Hari got out of the car and opened Marni's door.

'You will die in the desert if you do anything foolish,' he said, startling Marni so much she could only stare at him.

'Die?' she finally echoed weakly. 'But you're Hari, Nimr's brother, why would you want us to die?'

'I don't want you to die, I'm just telling you what would happen if you ran off into the desert,' he said, shifting uneasily, and looking anxiously towards the approaching vehicle. 'Fawzi will explain.'

'Have we been kidnapped?' Marni asked, and Hari looked even more embarrassed.

'Not for money,' he finally blurted out. 'We wouldn't do anything like that.'

'Is that supposed to make me feel better?' Marni demanded, but Hari had moved away from her and didn't reply.

The other vehicle was pulling up now, off the road but close enough for Marni to see it was a big four-wheel drive painted in the sandy camouflage colours of desert war vehicles.

'Here's Fawzi now,' Hari said, with such evident relief that Marni knew that whatever was going on, it was Fawzi who was the organiser— Hari was the weak link, should she and Tasnim need one.

'You're talking to her,' Fawzi said as he strode towards them. 'I said no communication.'

'But she asked—' Hari began.

'Bah!' his brother said. 'Just get her in the car and no talking. Where's Tasnim?'

'She's asleep.' Marni answered for the younger

brother. 'And she's eight months pregnant so whatever arrangements you've been making, I do hope you've got an obstetrician or a midwife on hand because an upset like this could bring on the birth any minute.'

Even in the dim light shed by the muted head-lights she could see Hari's face pale, but Fawzi only swore—well, Marni imagined he was swear-ing—and waved at his brother to get her into the bigger vehicle.

'No, I'll wake Tasnim and help her,' Marni said, thinking she could slide in beside Tasnim and they could both refuse to budge. She doubted the young men would drag them out forcefully, their inbred respect for women too powerful to overcome. 'You don't want her going into shock,' she added, for good measure.

Both brothers looked concerned this time, and Marni realised, whatever was going on, and whatever they intended doing, she could use Tas-nim's condition as a weapon against them.

Weapon! Was that a gun stuck in the belt of Fawzi's tunic?

If it was, then refusing to leave this car and get into the other one was no longer an option.

Marni frowned at him.

'Is that a gun?' she asked, and heard the incredulity in her voice.

He glanced down at it, telling her all she needed to know.

'Then hide it somewhere else on your person. The last thing Tasnim needs is to see people with guns!'

Especially young foolish people, she thought but didn't say.

The two young men began muttering at each other, Hari obviously getting more and more upset about the situation, but Fawzi seemed able to calm him in some way.

Marni slid back into the car and shook Tasnim awake.

'We've met up with Fawzi and have to get into his car,' she told the sleep-bewildered woman. 'I'm sure they don't intend to harm us because every time I mention your pregnancy they get worried. Let's just go along with things for now.

I'm here with you and I'll look after you, whatever happens.'

Tasnim's reaction was to burst into tears, which was hardly helpful, but eventually Marni got her transferred to the other vehicle, needing the help of both their kidnappers to get the heavily pregnant woman up into the high-set four-wheel drive.

Hari left them, no doubt to drive the limo back to the city, and Fawzi drove—carefully for one so young, Marni thought—across the desert, up and over sand dune after sand dune, reinforcing—as if she'd needed it—the desolation of the endless shifting sands.

Tasnim was asleep again and Marni dozed, aware there was no point in watching where they were going because it all looked exactly the same. Finally, he pulled up beside what looked like a small thatched cottage, half-buried in the sand.

'We are here. There is food and water, a little camping stove, beds and bedding. You will stay there. We will be watching you, though you may not see us. Just remember if you venture out into the desert, you will surely die.'

Marni didn't argue. Tired, confused and still

angry with Ghazi over his 'Why didn't you tell me' question, still hurt by it, she was beginning to think a comfortable prison cell might not be such a bad idea.

With Fawzi's help she got the still sleepy Tasnim out of the vehicle and into the little shelter, lit by two small gas lanterns that threw dark shadows into the corners of the room.

She could see a couple of mattresses against one wall, a pile of bedding in a corner, a table, where one lantern and a small gas stove, some plates and cups and a kettle stood, and a set of shelves packed with what was probably tinned food—the second lantern on the top of them.

'Lie down on that mattress,' she told Tasnim. 'I'll make you some mint tea. Assuming there is mint available for tea?'

She'd turned to Fawzi, hovering in the doorway, to ask the last question and a more hesitant or unhappy kidnapper she could not imagine.

'Of course,' he said abruptly, before walking out into the darkness. She heard the engine of his vehicle starting up then the noise gradually died away.

Tasnim was lying on the mattress, shivering in the night-cold desert air. Marni found a warm duvet and tucked it around the pregnant woman, thinking, as she did so, of her far-off obstetrics training.

How much did she remember?

'I'll get some tea,' she said. 'There might be biscuits. I'll have a look. We're quite safe here,' she added, reassuring both herself and Tasnim. 'And as soon as Ghazi realises we're missing, he'll find us.'

Given what had happened, she actually wasn't sure about that statement and had said it to reassure Tasnim.

It must have worked for Tasnim nodded and snuggled into the bedding. Satisfied that she was all right for the moment, Marni stood up to explore their temporary home. Water first, to boil for tea. Four large plastic containers of it suggested their kidnappers thought they might be here for a while. Fortunately, as she doubted she could lift a full container, she found a tap at the bottom of each of them so was able to slide a cup under it and get enough water to put into the kettle.

They'd thought of everything, she realised as she picked up a box of matches to light the little gas cooker. Beside the matches was a small gas firelighter but she was too tired to work out how to use it right now.

She set the kettle on to boil and began to check the shelves—sure enough, there were biscuits. Probably because the young men liked them, she decided, but she wasn't going to quibble over the reason for their choice.

Dried mint in a plastic container—she had no idea how much to use, having only made the tea with fresh mint when she'd been living in her little flat. She guessed amounts, realised there was no teapot so she waited until the water boiled then threw the mint into the kettle, adding sugar because that would help with shock.

But by the time she was done, Tasnim was asleep again, too deeply asleep for Marni to want to wake her.

Pouring herself a cup of tea, she carried it to the doorway of the hut, holding it in both hands as she sipped the sweet liquid, looking up at the billion bright stars and wondering if some combination or permutation of their movements had dictated the events of this most momentous day.

Well, at least you've achieved what you came to this place for, a cynical voice whispered in her head. Now perhaps you can get on with your life—go on dates, have some fun!

The realisation that she didn't want to go on dates—except perhaps with Ghazi—or have some fun—except, of course, with him—made her feel so miserable she gave up on the beauty of the night sky and crept back into the hut.

CHAPTER TEN

TASNIM WOKE UP irritable and unhappy, waking Marni, who'd settled on a second mattress nearby and had finally gone to sleep way past midnight.

'We have to get out of here,' Tasnim was saying, while Marni was still shaking off the heaviness of sleep. 'We've got to get away!'

'And go where?' Marni demanded, more concerned that she was going to have to find somewhere behind the shed to relieve herself in private.

And soon!

'If we walk out into that desert we're as good as dead,' she added, heading for the door then hesitating there. 'Do you think they're really watching us from somewhere? I mean, it's not as if we can escape, is it?'

'I went behind the shed,' Tasnim told her, guessing at her concern, 'not something that's easy when you're eight months pregnant. And I don't mean to walk out into the desert, but next time they come we'll have to overpower them some way and take the vehicle.'

I rather think that's a royal *we*, and she's meaning I will have to do the dirty work, Marni thought.

But right now she was beyond caring, hurrying around behind the shed, worrying now about how they'd wash themselves *and* their underwear.

Tasnim was ahead of her, for when Marni returned Tasnim had found a basin and filled it with warm water from the kettle, smelling of mint but very welcome nonetheless.

'I've found a couple of long gowns, like the men wear in the desert. I think the boys must use this place when they come out to hunt. They look clean enough so I'm going to have a wash and put one of them on. We can use the water we're washing in to wash our underwear.'

She must have read the surprise in Marni's face for she laughed and said, 'Being the descendant of a long line of desert women,' she reminded Marni, 'I know how precious water is. Out here we don't really need our underwear so we wash it this once then put it away until we're rescued.'

'Excuse me,' Marni said, 'but are you the same woman who was telling me, rather emotionally and only minutes ago, that we have to get out of here?'

Tasnim smiled at her.

'Pregnant women get very emotional,' she reminded Marni, 'but we're also very sensible under the hysteria because we've something very special to protect.' She patted her bulging belly. 'So now we have to be practical and look after ourselves, bathe and eat, and then we plan.'

The bathing and eating part went well, but planning? Tasnim's escape ideas became more and more impossible—finding a rock and hitting whoever came over the head, grabbing the gun, hiding in the sand then racing to the car while their kidnappers searched for them—until Marni grew tired of pointing out just why they wouldn't work.

'Well, we can't just sit here waiting to be rescued,' Tasnim complained. 'I mean, Yusef's still away, and is Ghazi likely to come looking for you?'

After the way she had stormed out of his office? Hardly!

But Marni didn't share that thought.

'Your staff will know you're missing and they must know you went off with Hari,' Marni said instead.

'Yes, but if Hari's not in town—if he's somewhere out here, watching us—how can they ask him where I am? And if they've really thought things through, that pair, they'll have come up with some reason why we didn't go home. They'd have told my people we were going to stay with one of the sisters or something.'

'Would your people believe them? I mean, you didn't pack anything or make any arrangements.'

Tasnim's smile was rueful.

'I do tend to be a little impulsive so although they might mutter among themselves, I doubt any of the staff would be surprised enough to be suspicious. And everyone always has spare clothes and toiletries, even make-up, for visitors. Like the stuff in your bedroom suite.'

They were sitting on Tasnim's mattress, and now she stretched out and lay down on it.

'I'm going to sleep for a while,' she said, patting Marni's leg where she still sat on the edge of the mattress. 'You keep thinking.'

Marni was relieved her companion was sleeping, but without Tasnim's chatter and flow of ideas there was nothing to stop Marni's mind drifting back to Ghazi and the events of the previous evening.

'They cannot just have vanished,' Ghazi yelled, striding about his office at the palace, glaring at his closest friends and advisors.

Unfortunately, deep down he believed they could have done just that. Marni, upset with him—hurt—over what had happened, or what he'd said, could have told Tasnim and Tasnim certainly had the guile and resources to hide them both away somewhere. In fact, the little devil would delight in the intrigue!

'I don't want to alarm you further—' Nimr's voice brought Ghazi out of his dark thoughts. '—but Alima says there's no way Tasnim would put her unborn child in jeopardy by doing something rash, and as far as Alima's concerned, leaving her home voluntarily at this stage of a pregnancy counts as rash.'

'So they *are* in danger!' Ghazi stormed, as his cousin swept away his last hope that Marni might be safe. 'Why? Who? Is it to get at me? Who have I offended?'

'At least we know they've got Hari with them,' Nimr offered, and Ghazi snorted.

'That's hardly comforting, Nimr. Those two young brothers of yours have about as much sense as the rabbits they love to hunt.' He hesitated for a moment, then added, 'Although, where's Fawzi? Maybe he knows something.'

Nimr shrugged.

'He went off a few days ago. Hunting, as you said. The pair of them are obsessed with all the old ways. They believe we should still live in tents and roam the desert sands—in the newest and biggest four-wheel drives, of course.'

Ghazi shook his head. He had no time to be thinking of Nimr's irresponsible brothers now, not when Marni was missing, perhaps in danger.

His gut had been tied in knots since he'd first tried to contact her at Tasnim's house, phoning when he'd been on his way from the hospital to Nimr's dinner, phoning again every ten minutes, feeling more and more desperate until someone finally admitted that neither woman had returned to the house.

If she'd left voluntarily it was because of him, and if something had happened to her, well, that was probably to do with him as well.

Somehow they got through their first full day of captivity, although Tasnim's mood swings took more out of Marni than the desert heat when she ventured outside during the day. Tasnim's first idea had been to write the word 'help' in big letters in the sand so the searching helicopter Ghazi was sure to send would see the message.

Although not believing for a minute Ghazi would send any form of rescue, Marni did write the word in large letters in the sand a few metres behind their shelter. But the wind that came up in the afternoon obliterated the word in seconds—*and* gave Tasnim a new idea.

'We'll put up a flag—use one of the wuzars in the pile of clothing.'

She dug around and produced a snowy-white length of material and Marni felt blood flowing into her cheeks as she realised it was the kind of undergarment Ghazi had shed on that memorable night.

Did Tasnim see that blush that she laughed and said, 'It's only a strip of cloth!'

As they'd agreed Tasnim should stay inside out of the sun, so as not to overheat, once again it was Marni who searched the dunes around their shelter for a stick long enough to hoist a flag.

But a flag with no message? Would it mean anything on the slim chance someone *did* come looking?

She found a stick behind the shelter where some small branches and bunches of dried grass had been stacked, presumably to provide fuel for a fire on a cold night. Digging around, wary of the scorpions Tasnim kept telling her to watch out for, she discovered another, smaller, though thicker stick. Taking it inside, she put the little gas lighter under one end of it, charring it all around so she could use it as a writing implement.

Tasnim objected to the word 'help' this time. It

had been chosen when Marni had written in the sand because it was shorter than the local word, but now they settled on the universal 'SOS'.

It took over an hour, charring the stick, writing, charring again, until it was done. But where to put it? Their shelter was nestled between dunes, and even on the stick and somehow attached to the roof, it would barely be seen above the sand.

'You'll just have to climb to the highest dune,' Tasnim told Marni, 'and if Fawzi and Hari really are watching us then you'll get caught but I don't think they'd shoot you.'

'Well, that's comforting,' Marni grumbled, although she was becoming used to Tasnim's cheerful fatalism.

Ghazi stared at Mazur in disbelief.

'You're telling me those two idiots are holding Tasnim and Marni because they want me to stand down and declare Nimr the ruler?'

Mazur shook the six-page letter he was holding.

'There's a lot more than that—all kinds of rot about you having stolen Nimr's birthright and brought shame to the family's name, and not having any honour or integrity or cultural importance.'

'What the hell is cultural importance?' Ghazi demanded, then shook his head at his stupidity. As if it mattered what the pair had said about him—the important thing was rescuing Tasnim and Marni, although Tasnim would probably be happier to see him than Marni would.

'Phone Nimr, get him here immediately. If anyone knows where those two reprobates might be holding the women, he should.'

Ghazi hoped he sounded more in control than he felt. His mind had been in chaos since Marni's disappearance, and now this! His chest was tight with worry, his gut knotted, and his neck ached with tension. It was bad enough that he'd hurt Marni with his thoughtless words, but to have put her into danger purely because of her connection to him—a connection he'd shamelessly used for his own purposes...

He'd kill those two.

'There are two or three old hunting shelters they use as bases when they're hunting.'

Nimr was striding into the room, his mobile

phone in his hand. He crossed to Ghazi and put an arm around his shoulder.

'I was in the palace when Mazur called. Man, I'm sorry about this. We'll get them back. The one thing we can he sure of, they won't hurt the women. They might be stupid and infantile in their pranks but they would never hurt a woman.'

Ghazi acknowledged his cousin's words with an abrupt nod, but Nimr's arrival had brought more than hope.

'Did you want the job?' Ghazi had to ask, although he'd been sure they'd discussed this many times and Nimr's answer had always been the same.

'No way,' Nimr assured him now. 'And those two lamebrains know that! I've told them times without number that I've other things I want to do with my life and, besides, I've always known, just as my father did, that you're the best man to rule our country at this time.'

He gave Ghazi another hug, then bent over the map he'd asked Mazur to find.

'A helicopter, flying low,' he suggested. 'I'll pilot it and you be the lookout. We'll take the little four-seater Bell. It can fly lower without disturbing the sand too much so we'll still be able to see.'

He nodded to Mazur, who left to arrange the helicopter while Nimr pored over the map then glanced up at Ghazi.

'What about Tasnim? How do you think she'll be holding up?' He grinned then added, 'Are your obstetric skills up to date?'

'Don't even think about it,' Ghazi said, watching as Nimr traced a line across the map with a red pen.

Obstetric skills? The words echoed in Ghazi's head.

Tasnim was eight months pregnant and had been through a major upset. He phoned the hospital and asked if they could have a midwife with her obstetrics bag standing by on the heliport in twenty minutes.

The little aircraft lifted lightly into the air, Nimr confident at the controls, Ghazi already working out logistics. He would send Marni, Tasnim and the nurse out on the first flight and Nimr could return for him.

Once they found the women…
If they found the women…

Marni had expected Tasnim to be asleep again
when she returned from planting her flag on the
dune. Tasnim dozed on and off all day because
her sleep at night was restless.

But Tasnim was awake—not only awake but
naked.

'There must be something in the clothes, either some kind of bug or they've been washed in
something that disagrees with my skin. Look!'

She pointed to where little red weals were
showing on her belly.

'They're itchy and they're driving me mad.'

Marni examined them, wishing she knew more
about general medicine than she did.

'They look more like an allergy than a bug of
some kind,' she said. 'And I've not been bitten
by anything. Lie down on the bed with just the
sheet on you and I'll see what there is in the sup-
plies that might help soothe the itches.'

Cold mint tea? she wondered.

But Tasmin refused to lie down, believing now

that whatever had bitten her could be in the mattress. She went outside and sat on the sand in the small amount of shade offered by their shelter, scratching at the weals and crying softly to herself.

Aware just how brave and held-together Tasnim had been so far, Marni knew she had to do something to help her friend before she fell apart.

She poured cold tea into a cup and tore a clean strip of cloth off a wuzar, then went outside.

'Let's try this to see if it helps, otherwise there's salt—we can try salt and water—or oil perhaps. She kept thinking of bicarbonate of soda, which had been Nelson's panacea for all ills. Bathing in it when she'd had chickenpox had definitely eased the itchiness. But their little hut didn't provide bicarbonate of soda…

And Nelson wasn't here…

Ignoring her own momentary weakness, Marni concentrated on Tasnim.

The rash was spreading, and Tasnim was getting more and more upset, undoubtedly because she was becoming more and more uncomfortable.

Ignoring the dune where she'd raised her flag,

Marni climbed another dune, back in the direction they'd come in from. Once at the top she shouted for the boys, alternating their names, yelling that Tasnim needed help, they had to come.

Her voice seemed a pitifully weak instrument out there in the vastness of the desert and she was certain they wouldn't hear her. She slid and slithered back down the dune, persuaded Tasnim to come inside and put on her own abaya, which she'd been wearing over her clothes when they'd been kidnapped.

Too tired and upset to argue, Tasnim dressed, then lay down to sleep—on the floor, not on a mattress.

She was still asleep when Manir heard the engine of a vehicle break the endless silence in which they'd lived since they'd reached the shelter.

'Come on, we're moving you,' Fawzi announced, when Marni met him outside the hut.

'Did you hear me calling? Tasnim's ill. She has a rash across her stomach and it could be affecting the baby. She needs to get back to town and see her doctor.'

'No can do,' Fawzi said, although Hari looked only too happy at the idea of getting rid of their captives. 'But it won't be much longer,' Fawzi continued. 'The imposter has our letter of demand and he'll be giving in any minute now.'

'The imposter? You mean Ghazi? Why is he an imposter?'

'Because he took the throne from our brother,' Hari said, apparently repeating a lesson Fawzi had drummed into him.

'But I heard Nimr didn't want the job,' Marni argued.

'He should still have taken it,' Fawzi said. 'It was his birthright.'

'Well, I don't understand the politics of your country and even if I did I'd have no right to comment, but it's silly to be standing out here in the heat. Tasnim's asleep so we can't leave yet, but if you move around the side into the shade I'll bring you some mint tea and biscuits.'

Hari, appearing only too happy to indulge in

tea and biscuits, led the way, and Fawzi followed, though, Marni felt, more reluctantly.

She set everything out on a makeshift tray and joined them in the shade, knowing it would be to their advantage if she could make friends with the young men, rather than hitting them on their heads with rocks.

And as they talked, relaxing quickly as young people did, she realised just how much they loved their country, especially the desert.

'I'll get some of Fawzi's photographs to show you,' Hari offered, when he'd finished his tea.

He raced over to the car, returning with a computer tablet, opening it up at a picture of an Arabian gazelle, a beautiful picture, taken so close up you could see the reflection of the camera in the animal's eyes.

'How on earth did you do that?' she asked, and Fawzi explained that they had many hides in the desert, like this place, only built for photography rather than for shelter.

'So you're still hunters, the two of you, but your gun is now a camera?' she said, and Fawzi looked pleased that she understood.

She slid her fingers across the screen, looking at one photograph after another, amazed at how good they were.

'You should put these into a book. I had no idea there was so much wildlife in the desert. It would be wonderful publicity for Ablezia.'

'This is what people are forgetting,' Hari said. 'That's what Fawzi and I don't like about the way our country is going. People move into the city and lose their interest in the desert, forgetting that the desert is part of their hearts and souls.'

'I can understand what you mean,' Marni said, but her visitors' attention had shifted from her, and as she watched the tension build in their bodies and their heads turn skywards, she heard the distant thud, thud, thud of a helicopter.

'It's Nimr, he's found us,' Hari said, looking as if he'd like to burrow deep into the sand and disappear.

'Quick, we have to leave!' Fawzi stood up and looked ready to flee but couldn't quite bring himself to haul Marni to her feet.

'Sit down again,' she said. 'You can't go rushing all over the desert with a helicopter chasing you. That's only for the movies and even in the movies the vehicle usually crashes. And there's no way on earth I'd let Tasnim get into the vehicle with you. She's too far gone in her pregnancy. Stay here, I'll talk to Nimr. I'll show him we're both quite all right and you've been very kind to us and that it's all just been a joke.'

'Except Fawzi wrote the letter to Ghazi, telling him we had you,' Hari reminded her.

'Well, we can get around that too,' Marni said above the now loud clatter of the helicopter rotors. 'Ghazi isn't going to throw you into a dungeon. In fact, I doubt he'll even throw you into jail. We'll work something out.'

She didn't add that he might well have given them a medal for getting rid of her, if his sister hadn't been involved as well.

Perhaps realising the futility of escape, the young men stayed put, all three of them bending their heads low over their knees as the sand from the rotors kicked up all around them.

The little aircraft touched down as lightly as a butterfly and when the engine was turned off and the rotors started spinning more slowly a door opened and not Nimr but Ghazi dropped onto the sand, followed by a woman with a large black bag and, finally, from the other side, Nimr.

'I'll kill you two,' Nimr roared, then proceeded to yell at them in their own language.

'Where's Tasnim?' Ghazi growled, anger in every line in his body, rage radiating from his pores.

Marni pointed towards the hut where a still sleepy Tasnim had appeared in the doorway.

Ghazi—although clad in jeans and a polo shirt there was no doubt from the way he held himself that he was Ghazi—led the nurse in that direction,

So that's what he thinks of me, Marni decided sadly.

Ghazi thought he'd held himself together quite well through the ordeal of not knowing where Marni was, or even if she was alive. But when he jumped out of the helicopter and saw her sitting on the sand, chatting happily to her kidnappers the tension that he'd held in check erupted into searing, white-hot anger.

Not wanting to let fly at her in front of so many people, he held it in check and sought out his sister instead, taking her in his arms and holding her close while she sobbed onto his shoulder. Her cries of relief were rising towards hysteria, her babbled words barely understandable. He soothed and comforted her, taking his time to calm her down before peeling her off his body so the nurse could check her.

By that time Nimr had joined the little group sitting on the sand, and they had obviously calmed him down because both his brothers were not only still alive but didn't seem to have been harmed in any way.

Ghazi walked towards the group and now, finally, the woman whose disappearance had nearly ripped his heart out looked up and nodded acknowledgement of his presence. She was pale, her hair coming loose from a plait and sticking out in all directions, but her face betrayed no hint of relief that they'd been rescued, or delight at seeing him.

'Nimr tells me the helicopter only carries four, Ghazi, so I think you should go with Tasnim bac to the hospital,' Marni said, so calmly he wanted to throttle her. 'I know you brought a nurse, but Tasnim's been really strong up until this morning when she came out in a rash across her belly. I vaguely remember something called PEP, poly-something eruption of pregnancy that can happen in the later months. I think that's all it is but she's getting very anxious and upset about it and is desperately worried that it could affect the baby. If you're with her, you'll be able to keep her calm until she gets back home and her own obstetrician sees her.'

Ghazi stared at the woman he'd come to rescue.

Was that all she had to say?

Apparently not, because she was speaking again.

'That way, I can get a ride back to town with Hari and Fawzi, or Nimr's said he'd be happy to fly back out to pick me up once he's dropped Tasnim off.'

She had it all organised, this pale, dishevelled devil he'd fallen in love with.

And not a *hello Ghazi, nice to see you, sorry if you've been worried* to be heard!

She was unbelievable and, heaven forbid, unbelievably beautiful to his eyes—even in an old kandora she must have found in the hut and smudges of exhaustion under her eyes.

Had he hurt her so much that she was treating him this way?

Like a passing stranger?

Or a *pretend* fiancé?

The pain in his gut suggested this might be so, but how could he say anything in front of Nimr and his brothers?

'Are you in agreement with this plan?' he asked Nimr.

His cousin nodded.

'I think Tasnim will need you as well as the nurse,' he said.

Knowing Nimr was probably right, Ghazi turned to the young men.

'As for you two,' Ghazi he said, 'can you be trusted to stay here with Marni until we return or will you get some other wild idea and take off again?'

'We'll be here,' Hari said, so promptly Ghazi

had to wonder what threats Nimr had already made to his brothers.

'I think we should go right now,' the nurse called from the doorway of the hut, and Ghazi, after one last, despairing look at the woman he loved, turned back to help his near-hysterical sister into the helicopter.

'Well, that went well,' Nimr said to him when they were airborne once again. 'Some little glitch along the road to matrimony?'

'Just keep flying,' Ghazi growled. 'And don't think for a minute you'll be flying back there, unless you want to ride home with your brothers—which might not be a bad idea. With you there, I'll be less likely to murder them.'

Nimr flew.

CHAPTER ELEVEN

NOT A PRIVATE word, not a touch—he hates me!

With Hari and Fawzi chattering on in their own language, Marni was left with her own gloomy thoughts.

You didn't exactly rush into his arms yourself, she reminded herself, which only made her feel even worse.

The problem was that, being the honourable man he was, Ghazi would undoubtedly feel he was bound to her in some way—apart from the pretend betrothal.

Enough to make the betrothal not pretend?

Probably, Marni decided gloomily, then became aware the other conversation had turned to English.

'Do you think Ghazi will banish us?' Fawzi was asking.

Marni studied the young men and saw fear and despair in their faces.

'I doubt that very much,' she said gently. 'You did a very silly thing but no harm has come of it. And you did it for reasons you believed in your hearts were right. I'm sure Ghazi will understand that.'

'You will speak to him on our behalf?' Hari begged, and although Marni knew her words would achieve little, given Ghazi's current opinion of her, she agreed that she would.

'But you'd do better speaking to him yourselves—apologising for causing alarm. And I think he'd be more willing to forgive you if you can come up with more than just an apology. What do the pair of you do, apart from kidnapping women?'

'We hunt,' came the chorused reply.

'Hunt animals for food?'

The young men laughed.

'No, for the camera,' Fawzi said. 'You saw the pictures, and that gun I had, well, it was an antique—no way would it harm anyone or anything. We love the old ways but some of our desert animals are almost extinct. Some we trap and keep to breed from—out at the old palace—then we set the young ones free when they are able to live on their own.'

'Your photographs are brilliant,' Marni told him, 'but would it not be better for people to see these animals and birds in the wild? Could you take tourists on trips to the desert—not just to eat dinner and watch the sunset, the way tourism operators do now, but run specialist tours for photographers and wildlife lovers. You could mix the old ways with the new, as tourists want comfort—set up luxury tents and provide good food. I am sure that kind of thing would really take off.'

She saw the growing excitement in their eyes so wasn't surprised when the talk again excluded her—not that she cared. If this pair could find something useful to do with their passion, they'd have no time to be thinking up wild schemes, like kidnapping pretend fiancées.

Which brought her thoughts back to Ghazi, but what he must be thinking she had absolutely no idea.

Flying the little aircraft was second nature to him. He and his boyhood friends and relations had been flipping around in them since they had been teenagers, so he had time to plan.

No matter that Marni might hate him, he had to do the right thing by her, his honour demanded that much. He'd sort out the rest later.

He phoned Mazur and gave him orders to have everything in readiness at the old palace, for that was where he'd take her—where he felt most at home, and where he knew she would be safe.

'I'll need someone qualified to marry us. With the photograph as proof of her grandfather's agreement to the betrothal, we won't need anyone to stand in place of her father, and I'll use Nimr's otherwise useless brothers as witnesses, then send them packing back to the city and deal with them later. I want my quarters prepared, clothing and toiletries for Marni, and food laid on, but no hovering servants. She'll need privacy and quiet, Mazur, to get over the ordeal she's suffered.'

He tried not to think about what would happen beyond the ceremony he was planning—what might happen in his quarters. He knew what he hoped would happen but feared he'd damaged the tender shoots of their relationship beyond repair, not with his lovemaking but with the rash words he'd uttered afterwards.

Nearly there, and now he saw the brave little flag flying from a dune beyond the shelter and knew she'd put it there. Kidnapped and left in the middle of the desert, she'd not only handled the situation but had done her best to get herself and Tasnim safely out of it.

He set the aircraft down, waited while the rotors slowed then dropped down to the ground.

Marni watched him walk towards them. Behind her, the two men stood, but she couldn't get her legs to move because this time Ghazi wasn't radiating anger. In fact, he appeared to be smiling and she was reasonably sure he wouldn't be smiling at Fawzi and Hari.

'You two get into your vehicle and get over to the old palace,' he said. 'I want you there as soon as possible. I've got a job for you to do.'

The pair looked shocked, but moved rapidly enough as Ghazi drew closer, his hand waving them away dismissively.

'But they wanted to talk to you about an idea

they've had,' Marni objected, with only the slightest quiver in her voice betraying just how trembly she was feeling inside now she knew she'd have to face Ghazi on his own—be with him on *her* own!

'They can put it in writing—Fawzi's good at that!' Ghazi growled, coming closer and closer to where she sat.

She feared if she stood up her legs would give way on her, because just seeing him was causing palpitations, and quivering nerves, and goose-bumps on her skin, and too may other physical sensations to name.

'You,' he said, putting out his hand and haul-ing her unceremoniously to her feet and march-ing with her towards the helicopter, 'are coming with me.'

'Do you think this is the modern equivalent of one of our ancestors throwing his woman over a camel and riding off into the desert?' Hari whis-pered to Fawzi, loudly enough to bring another growl from Ghazi.

'Is Fawzi right?' Marni asked, because she had

to say *something*. 'Are you throwing me over your camel and riding off with me?'

He had helped her into the helicopter and now stood outside, looking in at her.

'Would you like that?' he asked, his voice deep, his eyes, his face unreadable.

'I don't know,' she answered honestly.

Or was it honestly? she wondered as he marched around the chopper to get in behind the controls. She suspected that, somehow or other, she'd fallen in love with this man, without really knowing him at all.

Was that possible?

Or was it nothing more than the manifestation of the attraction that had flared between them from the beginning?

But would lust make her heart ache when she saw the tenderness with which he treated Safi?

Would it make her heart skitter when he smiled?

Not that there was any evidence of a smile at the moment. In fact, sneaking a sideways glance at him, she had to wonder if she'd ever see him smile again. Not any time soon, that was for sure.

'Are you all right?'

The demand came when they'd lifted into the air and banked as if to go even deeper into the desert.

She wanted to cry. Wanted to ask why he hadn't asked her that before. But he was all business, and she could do business.

'Desperately in need of a bath but apart from that, yes, I'm fine,' she said, and saw a slight frown mar the inscrutability of his expression, but it was quickly gone.

'You'll have time for a bath,' was all he said, or maybe he kept talking, but if he did, Marni missed it, too filled with astonishment at what lay ahead of them.

Rising out of the desert sands, barely perceptible at first, was what seemed like an immense building. High walls, sand coloured and seemingly endless, round turrets set at intervals, and where the walls changed direction, and within the walls, more walls, and domes, and spires.

'It looks as if it just grew up out of the desert sands like some fantastic plant.'

She breathed the words, lost in wonder as they

flew closer and the immensity of the old palace—
for that was all it could be—was revealed.

Now she could see colour—rugs hanging over
balcony parapets to air, market stalls set up inside the walls, the sun glinting off brass and silver pots and pipes and urns.

Ghazi circled the building, allowing Marni a
glimpse of an inner courtyard, green with trees
and plants, then landed on a concrete pad at the
back of the building but within the outer walls.

Speechless with astonishment and wonder,
Marni followed Ghazi as he led her past a long
row of stalls, with horses' heads poking out of
some—horses here, not cars—and further on
past different stalls—camels?—all the time heading towards the main building.

'You're late!' he said, as Mazur pulled up in a
little electric cart so they could ride the rest of
the way.

'You flew too fast,' Mazur countered, but when
Ghazi slid in beside him in the front, Mazur
clapped him on the shoulder.

'It's done?' Ghazi asked.

'All done, although Fawzi and Hari aren't here

yet. Not that it matters. All you need are two adult males.'

Ghazi nodded but gave no explanation of this weird conversation. Not that Marni minded. Now she was finally somewhere civilised, all she could think about was a bath. She just hoped this place was stocked up with clothes and underwear, because second in importance to the bath would be clean underwear!

They drove through an arch into the courtyard, a wonder of green in the barren land. All around the courtyard Marni could see arched openings that led into the shade of the wide loggia, the covered outside sitting area.

Mazur stopped the cart at the bottom of shallow steps, and Ghazi hopped out, turning to offer his hand to Marni. To her horror, she found that she was shaking—that the simple of touch of this man's hand had thrown her into a quivering mess.

She tried a smile and said weakly, 'I was doing fine up till now.'

He squeezed her fingers and she saw the familiar kindness in his eyes—kindness and something else she didn't recognise.

'You have been marvellous. Tasnim told me how you helped her remain calm.'

Marni shook her head, and tried a better smile.

'No, Tasnim did her bit. She told me it was the generations of desert women standing behind her that kept her going.'

Ghazi saw the bravery in her feeble smile and felt the tremors of post-traumatic shock shake her body. He wanted nothing more than to gather her into his arms and hold her close, tell her everything would be all right now—tell her things he barely understood himself.

But Mazur was there, servants appearing from inside the house, and a young woman, obviously chosen by his major domo here to look after Marni, was waiting in the doorway.

'This is Lila,' Mazur said, beckoning the woman forward. 'Lila, will you take Ms Graham to her suite and do whatever she needs you to do.'

So Ghazi had to hand Marni over to a stranger and hope she had the strength to keep going for just a little longer.

'Does the girl know what is planned?' he asked Mazur.

'Only that you wish to see Marni in the majlis in an hour.'

Ghazi heard the doubt in Mazur's voice—doubt and no little condemnation.

'I know she's exhausted but that's why I must do it now,' Ghazi told his friend. 'Once we're married she can rest.'

'Did you tell her?' Mazur demanded, and Ghazi shook his head, unable to explain that he hadn't been able to bring himself to mention marriage to Marni on the flight.

Because he was afraid she'd object? Refuse to go along with it?

'Then you should,' Mazur said firmly. 'I know you think you're doing the right thing, but you can't just drag the woman down the aisle with two witnesses—and why couldn't I be a witness might I ask?—and expect her to go along with marrying you.'

'It's for her safety and as for witnesses, she knows you and I need you to be there as her friend, not mine,' Ghazi snapped, then he strode away from his friend and mentor, angry, con-fused and heartsore.

'We must hurry,' Lila said as she led Marni along marble corridors and through jewelled archways, finally entering a room with a high domed ceiling, painted a deep, rich purple that matched the curtains around the huge four-poster bed.

'Why?' Marni managed to ask, as she took in the magnificence of this room, with its grilled windows looking out to the courtyard.

'Because we only have an hour. I have drawn a bath, it is all ready for you. I will wash your hair while you are in it, then perfume you and do just a little henna design on your hand because although no one is supposed to know, you will be marrying our prince today.'

'I will be *what*?' Marni demanded, the words muffled as she'd been pulling the long tunic off over her head as she spoke.

'Getting married,' Lila said, obviously very ex-cited about the upcoming event.

'No, and, no, and, no!' Marni stormed, although she did step into the bath. She could hardly argue with Ghazi stark naked—*dirty* and stark naked. 'I'll have the bath but I'll wash my hair myself and while I'm doing it you find whoever you have to talk to and get a message to your prince that I'll see him in my room in twenty minutes.'

'Oh, but you can't do that—not in your bedroom,' Lila protested.

'No?' Marni muttered. 'We'll see about that! You just get the message to him. And leave some underwear and something I can wear on the bed before you go.'

Sinking into the water, delicately scented and bubbling around her, was pure bliss, but having set her own deadline she couldn't lie back and enjoy it. She wet her hair and lathered it with shampoo that was handily placed on a shelf alongside the bath, rinsed it off and rubbed conditioner in, then let her hair absorb the treatment while she scrubbed her body clean of sand and dust and dirt.

Emptying the bath water, she stood up beneath the overhead shower and showered off the conditioner, then stepped out of the bath, wrapping herself in a super-soft towel and growing angrier by the minute that she hadn't been able to revel in the luxury of her first bath in three days.

The memory of when she'd last showered brought a rush of embarrassment, and she wondered if summoning Ghazi to her room might have been a mistake.

No! She had to talk to him. A pretend betrothal was one thing, but being rushed into marriage was just not on.

Wrapped in the towel, she went back into the bedroom, to gasp in wonder at the clothing Lila had apparently deemed suitable for her wedding.

Various packets of lacy underwear offered her a choice of colour and size, but it was the garment that would cover it that gave Marni pause. It was a simple enough gown, long and straight like the tunic she'd been wearing in the desert, but there any similarity ended, for this garment was apparently made with spun silver—fine and delicate silver—elaborately embroidered around the sleeves, neckline and hem.

It was something that should be in a museum, not about to be worn by any ordinary mortal.

She searched the walls of the bedroom, knowing there'd be concealed wardrobe and dressing room doors somewhere, and within those rooms there'd be other clothing—something else she could put on.

The doors eluded her, so she found underwear her size among the packets then returned to the bathroom, sure there'd be a robe there she could wear.

No such luck, but the towels were huge, and choosing a dry one she wrapped it around herself, then went across to a small sitting area by one of the windows to await her confrontation with her betrothed. Talking to him in the sitting area was slightly better than anywhere near the bed, but the bed still seemed to dominate the room.

And her thoughts!

Seeing her clad only in a towel was very nearly Ghazi's undoing. To hold her, smell her skin, feel her still damp hair against his face, peel off the towel—

'So, what's this all about?' the woman in the towel demanded, and he jerked his mind back to reality.

'No, don't bother answering that,' she added, before he could reply. 'It's your sense of chivalry, of honour that you're insisting on this marriage business. And sit down, I can't keep arguing with you when you're towering over me up there.'

For some reason he wanted to smile—perhaps because she should be at such a disadvantage in the towel, yet here she was issuing orders to him.

He didn't smile, knowing that would only make her angrier, but he did sit, and, sitting, could take in the clear pale skin of her shoulders—was that a bruise or the remnant of a love bite from the other night?—and the shadows of tiredness beneath her eyes.

His arms ached to hold her, to kiss away those shadows, to feel her body tight against his—where he was sure it belonged.

But was she sure it was where *she* belonged?

He had no idea, which was why he had to tread carefully.

'It's a matter of keeping you safe,' he said, forcing his mind to take control of his wayward thoughts. 'I need to have the right to protect you for as long as you remain in this country. As my wife, you would have a status that makes you, by tradition, untouchable. We don't have to stay married for ever or have a marriage in anything but name, but what has happened once could happen again, and next time your kidnappers could be more dangerous than a couple of stupid young men.'

She frowned at him and he wanted to wipe away that frown, to smooth the skin above her neat little nose, maybe kiss the frown away.

'They're not stupid, they just don't have enough to occupy them and that always leads to trouble with young people,' she said, and Ghazi was so lost in thoughts of kisses it took him a moment to catch up.

'You mean Hari and Fawzi? I've been telling Nimr that for ages, but we're not here to talk about them, surely?'

'Not exactly, but it's the same thing in another way. Those two, well, we've worked out what they can do—run wildlife safaris for photographers and animal lovers. But they did what they did because they could—because no one's ever said no to them or their wild schemes and I suspect it's just the same with you, no one's ever said no to you so you dream up this stupid idea of us getting married for whatever reason and don't stop to think what I might have to say to it.'

Now he did smile, and if the delicate flush of colour on her chest above the towel was any indication, he didn't think he'd made her angrier.

Marni had thought she was doing quite well with the conversation, considering she was sitting practically naked in front of the sexiest man in the world, and her thoughts were rampaging on about giving in to her body and letting the towel slip, and then he smiled and her mind went blank.

'What *do* you have to say to it?' he asked, the smile still lurking because she could see it shining in his eyes.

To what?

She'd totally lost the thread of the conversation, if it had ever had a thread.

And *she'd* summoned *him*, so presumably she was the one who was supposed to be in control.

'To us getting married,' he said in such a kindly manner she wanted to slap him—or perhaps kiss away the little quirk of a smile on the corners of his lips. 'After all, we are betrothed, and as I said earlier it needn't mean anything, but it would give me the right to protect you, Marni, and I think I owe that to your grandfather.'

'Pop! Oh, heavens, I'd forgotten all about Pop. I need to phone Nelson, I need to find out—'

Ghazi touched her gently on her knee.

'Your grandfather is doing well—far better than his surgeon expected. I have spoken to both the surgeon and to Nelson every day. It will be a long convalescence, as you already knew, but he's progressing extremely well.'

Marni wasn't sure if it was the assurance or the hand on her knee that brought a rush of relief to her body, and with the relief came a release of the tension she'd been feeling for days.

And a burst of gratitude to this man who thought of everything.

Except she didn't want to be feeling grateful to him—she didn't want to be feeling anything!

Not that she'd have a hope of stopping the physical stuff!

But right now she had to get past that and get

her brain working again, so she could explain why she wasn't going to marry him.

Wouldn't it be easier to just give in and marry the man? Then she could sleep.

Except...

'You say we're getting married so you can protect me but if I go back to being plain Marni Graham, a theatre sister, and live in a flat at the hospital, go to and from work there, then there'd be no need for protection. Now I know you better I know you can handle your sisters, so we can dispense with the betrothal business and everything can go back to normal.'

Her heart grew heavier and heavier as she spoke, yet she knew it was the right thing to do.

'Can it?' he asked, while the strength of the attraction between them was such that she could feel his body against hers, his mouth capturing her lips, although a full metre of palace air separated them.

'Of course it can,' Marni said, but the words didn't come out as strongly as she'd hoped they would. In fact, they sounded feeble in the extreme.

She took a deep breath and tried again.

'It's not only the protection thing that's pushing you,' she told him. 'I know you well enough to understand you feel you have to marry me because it's the honourable thing to do, and that's just nonsense. What happened happened, and I wanted it as much as you did.'

'What *happened* was that I hurt you,' Ghazi said, his voice full of regret. 'Hurt you with my foolish words, but it wasn't that you'd disappointed me in any way, but that, had I known—'

'You'd have pulled back,' Marni said. 'Don't bother denying it, it's happened to me before.'

The pain in her voice was too much! He stood up, lifted her out of the chair and sat down again with her on his knee. He brushed the hair back from her face and kissed her gently on the lips.

'Maybe,' he said, running his hand over her hair, enjoying just holding her, 'but only until I could make it special for you, make it easier and more enjoyable—slower and more careful, so it was more pleasure than pain for you. But how was I to know?'

He looked into her eyes, filmed with tears, although a brave smile was hovering around her lips.

'That I might still be a virgin at my age?' she asked. 'Not many people would think it. It wasn't that I was keeping myself for someone special, or that I thought my virginity precious, or anything that definite at all—it just happened.'

She was studying his face as she spoke, as if hoping to read understanding there.

'You see,' she continued, 'I was brought up by two elderly men, who loved me as dearly as I loved them, so early on, at school and university when all my friends were experimenting with sex, I couldn't quite get into it, afraid Pop and Nelson would be disappointed in me, that they'd think less of me. I knew if someone did come along that they'd like and approve of, then probably it would happen, but no one did, and then I was older and suddenly it was embarrassing to be a virgin and that made it harder and harder and—'

He cupped his hands around her face and kissed her gently on her lips.

'And when you did tell someone you thought might be the right man, he mocked you, hurt you with cruel words and snide remarks?'

She nodded and rested her forehead on his chest while he wound his fingers through her hair and held her close.

'So, now that's sorted,' he said, 'how about we go and get married so I can show you just how wonderful it can be?

Marni eased her head off his chest and looked at him.

'You could show me anyway,' she teased. 'The bed's right there, and no matter what you say, you're marrying me because you feel it's the honourable thing to do, aren't you?

He was and he wasn't but how to handle it?

Could he, who'd never opened up his heart to anyone, not even his closest friends, open himself up to this woman?

Couldn't that lead to loss of power?

To vulnerability?

To pain?

Yet, holding her, knowing her as he now did, he knew nothing less would do.

He stood up and put her back in her chair then knelt before her, taking both her hands in his.

'You're right about the honour,' he said, trying hard to get the words he needed—to get them right. 'Yes, I believe marrying you is the right thing to do, and even if you feel you don't need it, I want to be able to protect you—to protect you, provide for you and care for you.'

Deep breath because this was it—this was where he laid bare his soul.

So she could trample on it?

He had no idea.

'But most of all I want to marry you because I love you more than I have ever believed I could love anyone. These last few days have been the vilest kind of torture, because not only did I not know where you were, or even if you were still alive, but because I'd hurt you before we'd parted, and not knowing if I'd ever be able to explain— to make things right between us—well, that was the worst agony of all.'

Marni stared at him in utter astonishment.

'But you never said—'

'Did you?' he countered, smiling up at her in such a way she felt her entire body melting.

'How could I? I was worried it might just be lust, although as I got to know you, saw your kindness, your love for your country and your people, the way you were with Safi, it felt like love, but what did I know about that? It was as foreign to me as Ablezia, so how could I tell? I just wasn't sure.'

'Not I until I lost you,' he admitted, then he lifted her hands and kissed the backs of them, before turning them and pressing a kiss into each palm.

'So we're good to go?' he asked, his voice shaking just slightly with what could only be nerves.

'I guess so,' Marni told him, although she was sad that Pop wouldn't be there on her wedding day. But then she leaned towards him, ready for the kiss that *had* to be coming.

Needing the kiss as confirmation of their love.

'If that towel falls off, we'll never make the wedding,' Ghazi told her, not kissing her at all but standing up and stepping back, needing space between them so the fires didn't start up again. 'Get yourself dressed. I'll send Lila back to help you.'

He headed out the door

EPILOGUE

MARNI WALKED THROUGH the suite of rooms she'd chosen for Pop and Nelson, checking everything was in readiness. This suite had a small kitchenette and she'd stocked it with their favourite snacks, brands of tea and coffee, and a refrigerator full of cold drinks.

It would make Nelson feel more at home if he could prepare small meals for himself and Pop and, as Pop was still convalescent, they'd both appreciate not having to join the family for every meal.

'Stop fussing, it's perfect, and it's time to leave for the airport.'

Ghazi had obviously known where to find her and he stood behind her, slipping his arms around her, one hand resting protectively on her belly where the surprise she had for Pop was just beginning to show.

She leant back against her husband, aware of him in every fibre of her being, aware of the love that flooded through her whenever he was near.

In six short months her life had changed so tremendously it still had a dreamlike quality. She'd soon learned the wife of the ruler had a multitude of duties to perform, but his family had been wonderful, even Tasnim, with her new baby—Marni—was constantly on the phone.

Like him, she was still learning 'the job' but it was becoming easier every day—her reward for her diligence, the nights she spent in the arms of her lover—night after night of excitement, tenderness, raging lust and pure bliss.

Ablezia had certainly provided the answer to her 'virginity thing'!

'I can feel you thinking about sex,' Ghazi whispered in her ear.

'Not here, and there's no time anyway,' she told him, but she pressed her body against his and enjoyed the ripples of excitement even such a casual embrace could cause.

'We have to leave—the plane's due in within half an hour.'

She spun around and kissed him, her excitement over the arrival of Pop and Nelson now quelling other kinds of excitement.

Like most of the guest suites, this one opened onto the inner courtyard and Ghazi led her out that way and through the gardens to the garages at the back. This told her he'd be driving them to the airport—no driver for this private family meeting.

The courtyard seemed darker than usual, and only a few lights shone from the rooms around it, although usually the place was flooded with light.

'Austerity measures?' she teased, waving her hand towards the dark building.

'Probably a problem with a fitting somewhere,' Ghazi replied, 'and the electrician's closed off a whole section of the power.'

She forgot about it as they drove to the airport, although as they skirted the city, it, too, seemed to be less lit up. But Ghazi was talking about Safi, staying at the palace, in the harem, with his mother and younger brothers, awaiting his next operation.

One of Marni's projects was setting up a fund to raise money for the families of children who came to Ablezia for medical treatment—money that would allow family members to accompany the children and cover any loss of income they might suffer because of their absence from work back in their homeland.

They talked of it until they pulled up at the airport, driving to a private area where Ghazi's own plane would touch down.

Had touched down!

And there was Pop, using a walking stick but as upright as ever, Nelson right beside him, while a steward came behind them with their luggage.

Marni raced across the tarmac and threw her arms around her grandfather, tears coursing down her cheeks. She could feel his fragility as she held him, and that made her tears flow faster.

Eventually he eased away.

'See,' he said, 'that's why I sent you away. Couldn't have stood to have you weeping over me for six months. No more tears now. Say hello to Nelson then you'd better introduce this husband you seem to have picked up.'

Marni smiled through her tears and hugged Nelson, thanking him again and again for all he'd done, seeing Pop through his operation and recuperation.

'I know how difficult he can be,' she said, and Nelson smiled.

'And you also know I can handle him,' Nelson told her. He studied her for a moment then added, 'Ghazi being good to you, darling girl?'

Marni could only nod, the lump in her throat too big for speech. Then Ghazi was there, introducing himself, telling Nelson he remembered him, thanking them both for the gift they'd sent—the gift of Marni.

The steward had loaded the luggage into the car, and Ghazi seated Nelson beside him in the front, Marni and Pop in the back.

He drove slowly back towards the main road into the city, although maybe they were on another road for now all Marni could see that beyond the headlights was complete darkness.

'Is that desert out there?' Pop asked.

'Mostly, although this is a big highway and usually well lit.'

She'd barely spoken when the lights came on—and what lights! Strung between the tall lamp-posts were garlands of red and green, Christmas bells hanging from the centre of each one. The posts themselves were decorated with streamers, and along the road reindeer were picked out in fairy-lights.

'But you don't celebrate Christmas in Able-zia,' Marni protested, as more and more Christmas decorations came into view—huge banners hanging from high-rise buildings, streamers of coloured lights around the souk, Christmas trees in parks and gardens, and huge blow-up Santas atop any available chimney.

Ghazi slowed the car and turned back to look at her.

'I couldn't let you miss out on *your* celebration,' he said. 'Nimr took the idea to parliament, reminding everyone we have a lot of Western expats in our land. How better to welcome them and make them feel at home? he suggested. Then although Fawzi and Hari are busy with their safari plans, he got them busy organising it, seeing all the big corporations and explaining what we wanted.'

Marni shook her head, unable to speak for the wonder of what her husband and his people had done for her.

But the palace itself was even more breathtaking, for here everything was done in fairy-lights so the courtyard looked like a fairy wonderland, the tree in the majlis a miracle of silver decorations and tiny shining lights.

Still bemused by the whole thing, she showed Pop and Nelson to their suite, introducing them to the servant who would be on call for them at any time.

In Pop's bedroom they finally had time to pause, to hug each other again, and for them to study each other.

'How are you, really?' she asked, and he smiled his old, cheeky smile.

'Nearly there, my girl, nearly there. You know you can't keep an old dog down.'

Then the smile faded as he touched her cheek.

'And you? Are you happy? It's obvious he loves you, I can see it in his eyes. Do you love him?'

Marni smiled and hugged her grandfather again.

'With every breath I take, with every cell in my body,' she whispered, and Pop patted her on the back.

'That's good,' he said, then he held her at arm's length and she saw the twinkle in his eyes. 'So maybe two old men knew what they were doing, eh?'

'Happy?' Ghazi asked much later when she slid into bed beside him.

She shook her head and saw his frown. Kissed it away, and whispered, 'There has to be a better word than that for what I feel. Overwhelmed with love, that's what I feel, overwhelmed that you would do what you did for me tonight. You've given me so much with your love, and your trust, and bringing Pop and Nelson over for this visit, but to give me Christmas—that goes beyond everything I've ever known or expected or imagined.'

'So you *are* happy?' Ghazi pressed, as he gathered her into his arms.

'So far beyond it I can't explain, but maybe I can show you.'

And she did!

* * * * *